The girl in a pink bow

Pearl Sohal

BLUEROSE PUBLISHERS
India | U.K.

Copyright © Pearl Sohal 2025

All rights reserved by author. No part of this publication may be reproduced, stored in a retrieval system or transmitted in any form or by any means, electronic, mechanical, photocopying, recording or otherwise, without the prior permission of the author. Although every precaution has been taken to verify the accuracy of the information contained herein, the publisher assumes no responsibility for any errors or omissions. No liability is assumed for damages that may result from the use of information contained within.

BlueRose Publishers takes no responsibility for any damages, losses, or liabilities that may arise from the use or misuse of the information, products, or services provided in this publication.

For permissions requests or inquiries regarding this publication, please contact:

BLUEROSE PUBLISHERS
www.BlueRoseONE.com
info@bluerosepublishers.com
+91 8882 898 898
+4407342408967

ISBN: 978-93-7018-359-9

Cover Design: Shubham Verma
Typesetting: Sagar

First Edition: May 2025

This book contains mature themes, explicit sexual content, and adult language. It is intended for readers aged 18 and above. Reader discretion is advised.

Alcohol consumption and cigarette smoking are harmful to your health. This book in no way promotes the consumption of alcohol or smoking cigarettes.

Chapter 1

The aroma of freshly baked Vanilla Croissants on a bright summer morning is the kind of tease that a famished stomach appreciates the most after a swim in the ocean. Maohi was happily trotting the Italian streets, which led to a beautiful French bakery on the cliff adjacent to a white sand beach surrounded by turquoise water. She suddenly started getting honked at by a giant yellow tourist bus. Peepeee…pprrrnnn….. ppprrnnnn…. trrrn… trrrnnn…. Snooze! She woke up on a gloomy fall morning to realise that it had poured all night, and now her commute to work was going to be painful. The weather outside impacted her mental state significantly, and a friend of Maohi's defined rains as "personal hell". Maohi is running late, and Hyderabad traffic on a rainy day isn't the best way to start the day. She booked her cab before getting into the shower. There was a priority list to soap her body parts, and to what extent the list was completed depended on the cab driver's first notification. Sometimes, her feet wouldn't have their morning romance with the loofah for days. Most mornings, she would skip her breakfast, most important meal of the day, and would rely on coffee.

Our bodies and minds have worked all our lives to keep us alive, and we need to repay them. It's very important to have a symbiotic relationship with ourselves. If we keep exploiting our body and externalise our life, then we would become parasites to our system. Living off of our body cells while serving unnecessary social obligations. Our body and mind always tell us what is it that they need and it's a privilege to have the bandwidth to be able to listen to it. As long as our life isn't a fight for heat, nourishment and oxygen, we all have that privilege but seldom have the clarity to recognize it.

Most of her days in Hyderabad were spent working hard and partying harder. Our 20s aren't the age to indulge in the importance of things like a sound mind in a sound body. The exposure that we get and the life that we live in our 20s are probably the most cherished years of our adulthood. Abusing her body to push its limits and realise its potential was a necessary part of the journey.

It was a struggle for Maohi to find a place that she could call home in a city that she had never visited before. During the first 6 months of her professional life, she flew back home every month. Maohi would go apartment hunting every weekend, only to come back disappointed to an apartment she had started to despise. Brokers would promise her the stars, but she would end up in "Dumps". She eventually gave up on the brokers and took matters into her own control. Maohi started leveraging social media to reach out to people who were seeking flatmates or their replacements. After visiting almost 100 weird houses, from kitchen sinks being clogged for what seemed like days to the shabbiest people living in a clutter of garments, she landed at Kay Towers. The moment she stepped in, Maohi was welcomed by a beautiful girl in a sun-bathed apartment on the 27th floor. The apartment had huge glass windows for walls, and Maohi's room had the same huge windows with a view of the pool and the city lights. She saw her first sunset in Hyderabad and saw the sky change its colors. She knew she had found her home. She knew that the next few years of her life in this apartment were going to be some of her best years.

Adapting is a natural process, no matter how much we try to expel the change from our system, but as soon as we have a fair trade-off to deal with the change, we give in and eventually adapt to our new circumstances. In this process, we always get to experience ourselves in a way that we haven't ever before, and something within evolves. The realisation that now she had 2 homes came with a sense of unease. Maohi knew she would never be fully satisfied and that a part of her would always long for one home of the two. Only eventually in life would she realize that she wasn't meant to feel at home in only 2 places; the number would keep increasing because the Centaurus in her would keep her from settling.

Few romantic relationships came knocking on Maohi's door, and the one that stayed the longest, Aleb, quite literally knocked on her apartment door. The apartment bell wasn't functioning, but she heard a knock on the door. On receiving the visitor, she was informed that her flatmate had put up her table for sale on the Tower's internal portal. Maohi's parents had come to help her move and had just left. Her father had told her earlier that day that someone had come looking for the table. She assumed him to be the same guy and asked him to give his number so that he didn't have to keep visiting to find out about the table. With her parents gone and both her flatmates travelling, Maohi was having a rough night. She was contemplating if all the loneliness was worth it. The stranger that came knocking settled her nerves from the turmoil that she was enduring.

A turbulent feminine energy can be easily comforted just by coming into the presence of a secure and positive masculine energy. It's good to be independent in every way that you want to be, and it's not at all advised to rely on anyone else. Being self-sufficient is like an unsaid rule in this century. This process has made our lives so difficult that we are constantly hustling, and hence, it's almost impossible to accommodate any liability in our lives. Any kind of symbiotic relationship, not necessarily romantic, makes life easier, but these relationships are fragile. There is an exchange of favours in every relationship because the other person caters to a need that you haven't been able to cater to yourself. Once you form a habit of this missing piece of the puzzle, you end up getting attached. No matter how healthy a relationship is, the role of who is a liability keeps oscillating and it takes that one moment where a liability is made to feel like one because the other person doesn't have the bandwidth to accommodate. And in that moment, the bitter taste that it leaves lasts longer than we anticipate because we don't have the time to acknowledge it and never have a healthy discussion around it. That being said, there is no bigger joy than being able to be in your feminine energy around a positive masculine energy that has the maturity to provide you with the necessary romantic intimacy in its rawest form. On most days, it could be sexual but then there are days when this intimacy is just a natural flow of energy between a yin and a yang (I leave it on you to decide which energy of the 2 is the yin). Feeling complete in that moment comes as naturally as procreation comes to animals when they are of age.

We need to have the confidence to be able to start a new life all by ourselves. Even if we end up being in an alien world, without any way to communicate, we just need to know that we will be fine no matter what. It's very important to stay relevant and have the ability to manage our lives all by ourselves, but it's borderline unfortunate if we actually have to practise it. Being all by ourselves is very important to understand who we are and how complete we are as is; only then would we know what we need in a partner to complement us. To identify the frequency that resonates, we need to fine-tune our wavelengths (yes, plural). Once we are in that space, only then should we open ourselves to finding a relevant partner so that it's for the sake of joy and enjoying life and not because we aren't complete as is.

Living in Hyderabad helped Maohi explore herself and identify her capabilities as an individual. Her work wasn't demanding, but she wasn't getting the right opportunity. Her interest lay in front-end development as she was fond of art. She enjoyed website designing and studying about colors, fonts, the golden ratio, etc. Maohi researched colors and attended a 2-day lecture on the influence of colors on our life. Her fascination with the selection of colors grew after that lecture. Even though Maohi didn't get her desired line of work, she did manage to deliver as required. In no way was she a top performer, but she figured her way around. She did feel bad about not being able to succeed in her professional life, even though she gave it her all. She knew her heart wasn't in her work, and she wasn't the one to just "make it work".

The journey of finding ourselves is the most important journey that we can embark on. Our 20s are the perfect time for us to experiment with our professional, personal and love life. Listen to our gut and grab onto every opportunity that it approves of. Even though our brain is very sharp and we have access to a lot of data, relying on our intuition instead of the math in our head makes more sense. Our gut computes the situation based on what information we gather from our genes. Our body probably comprises a lot of information that might have been transferred from generation to generation and can probably date back to Adam and Eve (if you believe in God) or single-cell organisms (if you believe in science) or either (if you believe in both). The information transferred in the form of what color our eyes would be is very evident, but Maohi believed that our intuition or "THE GUT FEELING" is information transfer of years and years of experience and decision making. Irrespective of how much data our brain has been exposed to and the information it can process, it still is nothing as compared to years and years of experience and decision-making that resides in our system in the form of genetic data. Our intuition is the only guiding light that we need; we just need to actively use our brain and clear out the unnecessary noise so we can hear ourselves clearly.

Chapter - 2

Maohi fell in love with Hyderabad, or maybe she fell in love in Hyderabad, not sure what it was- but Hyderabad became her home. There is something about experiencing all seasons in a new city, and once we have experienced all seasons and the cycle starts all over again, it starts to feel familiar, and that excited electron jumps back to its original shell. She felt settled, if not fulfilled, in her job and apartment. Eventually, all of it started to feel amazing. Maohi was starting to love Hyderabad rains. Somehow, the raindrops were fuller and more wholesome. Not sure if that's how she started to feel within, or was it that the city poured with drops of larger circumference. She enjoyed every bit of being in that city and exploring it. Maohi would go out on dates, exploring new restaurants and going on drives exploring new routes and areas in and around Hyderabad. She took a trip to Gokarna, and it turned out to be the best experience of her life. She slept on the beach under the stars and woke up to the sound of waves. She hadn't felt as alive, for a good few years, as she felt on this trip. It also included incidents of stupidity, like getting tossed around in the rocks by the waves. Maohi took the trip with 4 of her friends. One of her flatmates, Shien, accompanied her, and the other 3 boys were her romantic interest, Aleb and his 2 friends, Rahul and Abrol. The first night, no one pitched the tent on the beach and so they all slept on a tarp. A snorting bull came out of the trees from the bushes behind them in the middle of the night. On hearing the noise, Abrol went from horizontal to vertical like a roller coaster in a split second. He ran towards the ocean while Rahul and Aleb tried to protect Shien and Maohi. It was as heroic as period dramas based on the 16th century and as romantic as Ashton Kutcher rom-coms. The next morning, they all woke up to a bunch of foreigners doing yoga next to them. Maohi, Shien and Aleb joined them and attempted a few asanas. Eventually, everyone took a dip in the ocean before eating pancakes. Shien and Maohi went bikini shopping in a small roadside shop.

Before their hike to the virgin beach, they were warned about a cheetah residing in the hill they were supposed to hike through, and the hill welcomed them with the recently shed skin of a huge snake. Their ascent mirrored the beginning of a thriller in the woods full of cannibals. But as they climbed and reached the top, it started to feel more like a chapter on "Live, laugh, love". Maohi's eyes sparkled when she looked at the turquoise water from the hilltop, the water was sparkling from the reflection of the sun rays. She had always been a water baby and the tropical climate did wonders to her skin, hair and mood. She went down, running with Aleb right behind her. She wore

The girl in a pink bow

a rucksack on her shoulder, which came in handy for Aleb to keep her from bruising her behind. Every time Maohi slipped, he pulled her up with the bag on her back and broke the fall. They all pitched their tents and then got into the water. Aleb asked Maohi if she would like to go to the other side of the shore. Maohi agreed and started to swim towards the other end. Only to eventually find herself being tossed around in the rocks. She assumed this was it and almost saw the light. She shut her eyes and laughed to herself, thinking, "Is this how I go?" "Have I been this stupid all my life?" Luckily, Abrol called out to her to check if she needed help and eventually pulled her out of her misery, quite literally. The moment Maohi rested on a rock and felt relieved, she realised that one of her boobs had popped out of her bikini during her struggle in the rocks.

Even though she felt fulfilled throughout that experience, she felt empty within. Maohi knew that Aleb had a thing for her but he was too into himself and wanting to have the time of his life. She felt the need for attention from time to time, but everyone was so busy living their own experiences that no one bothered. Everything was beautiful, and she felt ecstatic, but this need to feel important to someone kept creeping in.

Such episodes in our lives lead to revelations that we are constantly exploring ourselves through these experiences. We consciously need to register our emotions for the sake of our self-awareness. On most days, we are made to feel that wanting attention is incorrect and that we should be self-sufficient. Seeking random attention for validation isn't a healthy way of life, but wanting to be desired by our partner is essential. However, the need to be self-sufficient is paramount so that we don't surrender to an undeserving lot just to feel desired. Call it the paradox of need vs want.

Post Gokarna, Maohi started to prepare for her GMAT; an MBA was another milestone that had to be crossed just like Engineering. The major motivation around writing GMAT was to get an out. Maohi completed her bachelor's in information and technology and got hired as a software consultant for a consulting firm in Hyderabad. This was the first time that she was moving out from her house and she was looking forward to it to say the least. The decision to take up that role was fairly hasty and unplanned.

Maohi fell in love easily and let love guide her decision-making. The boy that she was dating during her undergraduate years had her convinced to move with him to Canada. Canadian Embassy to a Punjabi is what IIT is to every engineering student in Kota. She wasn't focusing on her placement drives but instead on writing IELTS so she could move with him. Their parents knew about them, and Maohi and Shard were to get married, so it was only natural for her to plan her life with Shard. Only to realize that he did not manage to complete his degree on time. No surprises there, and she had to find a last-minute fix to do something with her life because moving to Canada wasn't an option anymore. While she was struggling to get herself placed because she had missed most of her chances during her IELTS preparation, she found out that Shard had been going behind her back all this time. He had been manipulating and lying to Maohi. He never had an affair, and he intended to marry her, but he still chose to fool around behind her back, which broke her.

The girl in a pink bow

Happiness elevates your experience of life, but grief brings out our true selves, for in grief, our lenses are not tainted with unnecessary filters. Even though she was miserable, there were phases of reflection and introspection which made it clear why it couldn't have worked. There is a lot of potential in all of us, but love is a very consuming feeling. We tend to converge all our decisions in the direction of our partner and the relationship. We forget what it feels like to be the centre of our own world. We aren't the centre of "THE" universe; that's more like projecting and having expectations, but it's very important to identify that we are the centre of "OUR" universe. Our world revolves around us, and our sun rises and sets for us. A sense of importance helps give substance to our character, whereas a sense of entitlement makes us needy and petty.

Moving on is one of the toughest things in the world. Being with someone for years and then suddenly having to choose to live the rest of our life without them is atrocious. Hyderabad happened at the right time for Maohi, and she had the chance to move to a new city. Living in the same environment makes it harder to forget your ex because there are too many memories. Your brain doesn't comprehend why things or places around you don't feel the same as they used to.

Though he followed her to Hyderabad and tried to find a way to sustain, Maohi just didn't have it in her to appreciate his efforts anymore. She felt bad for him, but she just couldn't look at him the same way again. He would read "The Hindu" for the job interviews in Hyderabad while she would be working on "Economics Times" for her training assignments. She would get ready and leave for work, and he would get ready to go for the walk-in interviews. It could have been perfect, and that's what she wanted, but just a minor glitch and something that she dreamt about had become her living nightmare. She wanted him to just leave so she could get on with her moving on because just like the person he had Maohi believing he was, didn't exist, similarly the girl that he had fallen in love with didn't exist. His girlfriend died the day she saw his phone screen flash with a girl's name and post the call, he lied that it was his dad.

We fall in love with the idea of who they are and it's our fault that we believe there is potential. But to be fair to ourselves, we are led to believe most of the things through trickery only to be called *delulu*, eventually. Our delusions come from a place of wishful thinking and this wishful thinking is fuelled by all the lies that were told to us in order to woo us.

Hyderabad was a breath of fresh air; it was alienating at times, and Maohi would weep at least once every week! On most days she wanted to run back home but she kept telling herself to go one more day without losing her shit. There were days she would struggle to keep it together just because she'd faced a minor inconvenience during laundry day. Maohi was distracted on most days because of work, but every time she'd hit the bed, she'd get lonely and shed a tear. That's when she started drinking. We probably need 1 bad habit to replace another, and maybe that's the reason that whenever we retrospect, we do find one habit (addiction might be too strong a word) that made us feel alive but probably wasn't the best thing for a functional adult to have in life. Maybe we all are dysfunctional at most times in our lives, and these not-so-good habits help justify that. Luckily, all this drama unfolded in the first 6 months of moving to Hyderabad and before finding "Kay Towers" - a place Maohi would call home all her life!

Towers were where she found her first home; every article of the 2nd room on the right of the apartment P-2702 was a reflection of who she was. While she was living with her parents, she rarely got to experience herself and explore who she was. But now, she could just be what she wanted to be and express herself through every inch of her surroundings. The more she learnt about herself, the more she learnt about her happiness.

It's crucial for us to create a space for ourselves where we can be what and who we want to be. Experiencing ourselves in various forms and shapes helps in self-awareness.

Towers did not only give her a home, but it also gave her love. A new lover is very similar to moving into a new house. We have to unpack our baggage slowly, we have to identify how much space the other person is willing to create for us and so we unpack one thing at a time as the relationship progresses. If lovers are like new homes, then flings are like hotel rooms; we just have to unpack enough to scratch the surface. Which is enough for the necessary emotional and mental stimulation, provided the intimacy feels organic. We just have to go deep enough to identify if our hygiene (figuratively and literally) factors resonate.

Chapter - 3

We are blessed to have a mind and the tools to experience life in different ways, yet we choose to not exploit the potential of the system but instead let the system exploit our potential. The cerebral potential of humans is considered superior to that of animals, and yet we fail to identify how and when we all start to fall into the rat race. The system needs most of us to be disciplined and monotonous for the sake of the rest. There is this one socially accepted idea of perfection that most of us strive to achieve. This perfect human avatar is created to work like a bot and maximise the world's efficiency and grow GDP. Just because there is a standard that defines bad from good or normal from abnormal, we tend to lose our uniqueness in order to fit in. We start fixing pieces of ourselves that make us special to try and reach the gold standard. If we keep carving our rough edges, there will be millions and millions of "us" but none of "you" and "I" left. We need to nurture our uniqueness to reach our full potential and not carve ourselves into an acceptable average. It's a scary world, and we all have our insecurities that keep us from dreaming and choosing to be ourselves. Every single piece of what makes you "you" is fragile and essential and needs to be preserved.

Maohi had fallen in the same trap of the hamster wheel. She frequently switched jobs when she was in Hyderabad, and it was to try and find her calling. Her last switch in Hyderabad was into a solar start-up. She knew that she wasn't meant for technical roles and was more inclined towards functional roles. Also, for as long as she could remember, her answer to the question "What would I do if I became the Prime Minister?" was "I would create the largest solar power plant of the world in the Thar Desert". She always wanted to become an environmental lawyer or an environmental scientist. But like every other Indian household child in the 2000s, she was asked to take up engineering to become a software developer. Hence, the fish started its journey of trying to climb the tree and letting the monkeys and sloths intimidate her.

While at it during her college years, she never really learnt much about the world of software development but she did learn a lot about diversity that a small unit, like an educational institute, could reflect. So when Maohi decided to leave her technical role behind for a functional position in the solar industry, she found it very challenging, to say the least. It is fairly difficult for a North Indian to be completely accepted in a Southern region, and it got even worse when Maohi chose to take up a role in a male-dominant environment. The activity of Solar Module installation happens on the sites that are on the outskirts of the city. It was never considered safe for Maohi to be stationed at these sites with all the staff being males. She craved the relevant exposure to these sites whenever she heard people around her speak about the completion of a project, but she was never given an opportunity to visit these remote locations and experience the process in person. So, she chose to put all her effort and energy into excelling at her desk job. Once Maohi started to get confident about her work, and it started to reflect in her daily functioning, it began to intimidate her superiors a little. One day, when Maohi was sitting and working on her agreements to highlight any upcoming delay in the project completion, a superior randomly threw a question at her "At what angle and how deep should a pole be dug into the soil to withstand the solar module and have maximum exposure to the sun?". Maohi didn't know the answer to the question but she knew that an imaginary pole had started to bother someone's behind. Although her theoretical knowledge was good, this sort of data gets engraved in our memory mostly when we have had the chance to be present when the foundations are being laid down. The moment she started to feel fulfilled in her professional life, she was again reminded how she would always be restricted if she continued to be in an environment like this. How masculinity would have leverage over her. Maohi was never the one to play victim. She started to look for other opportunities that would be more relevant for her career graph. She was trying to understand the right move forward, whether within Solar power generation or outside. She enjoyed hearing about projects being commissioned that were coordinated by her from the inception to electricity generation. But that wasn't enough for her to consider admin work just to stay put in Solar.

The girl in a pink bow

Maohi soon started to catch on to the unnecessary resentment towards her when her superior started to instruct her colleagues in the firm to stay away from her, and the frequency of technical questions (irrelevant to her work) started to increase, just to let her down in front of an audience. She had a mind of her own, so no one could make her walk in a straight line, which didn't sit well with most. She needed someone to show her the direction, but she preferred using her own tools to carve the way. An environment where she was instructed to the "t" felt suffocating. Maohi was seldom applauded for wanting to do things her way. On the days she failed, Maohi was ridiculed, and on the days she succeeded, she was criticised by wounded male egos. Though she was enjoying her work, she eventually started to get excluded from the projects by her superiors. Her superiors would copy her style of work, which she had developed over time through her prior experience and exposure, and yet exclude her so they didn't feel like they were working on borrowed intelligence.

The solar industry was being supported by the government through subsidies and tax benefits in the early 2000s, but as new entities started to sprout, the benefits started to decrease. With "anti-dumping" policies (cheaper products from other countries are accompanied with heavy duties to allow indian markets to grow and reduce the competition from the imported goods), the cost of establishing a solar plant went significantly up. This was around the time when Maohi had strategized the installation of the solar rooftop plants. Maohi's company had won a government tender to install the solar plants on the rooftops of government buildings, but with this news of the "anti dumping" policy, the entire project was going to take a hit since the bid number wasn't making business sense. This stirred up frustration and paranoia in her superiors, and it started to worsen Maohi's work life. Maohi's unconventional ideas to handle the situation did not receive any acceptance. The firm was relying on the Government to exclude the anti-dumping rules for the procurement of solar modules for the projects initiated before the policy. It's good to be hopeful, but hope isn't a strategy. One fine day, Maohi lost her calm, and she entered the office building with her resignation mail saved in her outbox. Her resignation mail had a 10-pointer list against her immediate superior, and she had a colleague, one of her confidants, who proofread it. It was suggested to bring down the list of email IDs cc'd in the mail, which she did. Her discussion with the HR was fairly limited; she stepped out and went for a long walk to calm her nerves and finally breathed some fresh air. Relief had not filled Maohi's lungs the way it did today. Only when the weight started to lift did she realise how heavy her heart had grown in the past few months. She felt a truckload of cement being lifted off of her chest.

Maohi's heart kept shuttling between relief and agony. Though she was relieved that she had let go of a toxic work environment, it was agonising to be jobless at the same time. She was grateful to feel secure as her parents happily agreed to support her until she found her next stint. She had started to prepare for her MBA applications while hunting for a job.

When she was neck deep into her preparations, she received a call from her ex-colleague about an opportunity in Bangalore. This was around the time when Maohi's Boyfriend, Aleb, was also looking to switch cities. He was interviewing in Bombay and Bangalore for a new position. She decided to go ahead with the interview in Bangalore and closed a fair deal for herself. She was going to move within a month..

Maohi was hopeful that Aleb would land a job in Bangalore. Even if he didn't, it wasn't like he had started seeking out positions after consulting Maohi. If Aleb was willing to relocate for his professional growth, Maohi felt it was fair for her to prioritise her professional life as well. Corporates might feel thankless, but our relationship with our professional life is fulfilling, even if the nature of work is not. If you put in hard work, then you at least get some financial benefits. It might not be enough for the human spirit to thrive on, but it's still better than toxic relationships that only exhaust you and leave you feeling empty. On most days, it's not even our partner's doing but also our relationship with our romantic life, which is complicated, to say the least. Maohi oscillated between a passionate lover and an aspiring professional. To be both at once, it takes a very fulfilling job and an even more understanding partner. She knew that their relationship was going downhill, and this move to Bangalore, if it was without him, would be the final nail in the coffin. Aleb's mother wouldn't have approved of Maohi. His mother had started to look out for girls for Aleb to get married to. Even before she moved, he was already speaking to a girl he was introduced to by his mother. After 3 years of living in Hyderabad, when the day arrived, Aleb wasn't even with her to help her relocate. Maohi's old friend Vinek, who was working in Bangalore, came to get her from Hyderabad.

Vinek and Ankit were Maohi's friends from when she moved to Hyderabad. They were the first of her friends in a new city. Maohi, Vinek and Ankit became close friends from the time they shared their first bottle of whisky on the second day of work to celebrate the commencement of their professional lives. Since then, they just grew fonder of each other, and time only brought them closer. When Maohi switched companies and Aleb came into her life, her interaction with them decreased. She tried to meet them as often as possible, but she had to prioritise her boy and her professional life. It was on the day of her moving that she realised how blessed she was to have earned such lovely friends.

Chapter- 4

Tear-stained cheeks and a mouth full of pancakes was Maohi's first morning in Bangalore. The weather in Bangalore compensates for the stressful traffic it has to offer. Maohi was taken to a cafe by Vinek and though it was a beautiful spring morning, her heart was troubled. It was one of those days in her life where even the brightest shade of yellow looked grey and she felt blue. She was sitting in the sun trying to stuff down bacon pancakes with an Americano. She felt gloomier within because of the fear of having to start her life all over again in a new city. She knew she figured it out the first time and would manage it again. No matter how confident she felt, the soft, scared and fragile feminine element just wanted to give in and curl up inside a protective shell. Maohi thought this was probably how the crabs feel when they outgrow their shells and have to go looking for a new one. Transformations are necessary, but on most occasions, it's just outgrowing our shell and having to look for another one. Maohi knew this transformation wasn't her metamorphosis. Catharsis is an essential part for a human before experiencing the liberation of a butterfly. It takes time to find your space and time to be able to build your cocoon and corporate lives do not permit that kind of personal bandwidth. Maohi knew she would have to build her home all over again before she could feel the comfort of familiarity and sense of belonging.

Maohi reached the apartment in the evening that she had finalised through the information posted about it on the web. The apartment on the 24th floor was glorious and fairly close to her office. It was prettier than the one she had in Hyderabad, the room that she was to take up had 2 glass walls with a beautiful view of the city and her own private balcony. Though she loved the house, she felt that the energy of the house was a little off. Whether it was the people in the house or the gloom in her heart, she wasn't sure. She just knew that this wasn't the place that she was ready to move into yet. Maohi was added to the house's group chat and by evening, she had tons of messages from her future flatmates. She went through the group chat only to find out that her body was sensitive to the negative energy in the house. The girls in the house were arguing about the amount to be settled by the girl who had to move out. The conversations were so curt and inconsiderate that any house, no matter how pretty, could never feel like home in such a hostile environment. Maohi broke down as now she was in a new city without a house to move into. The only saving grace, her excitement to move into a pretty room and decorate it, did not exist anymore. She decided to call her mother to help her find apartments as she had work and had to go apartment hunting post-work in a completely new city. She shortlisted a few apartments and visited them with her mother. Hunting apartments in Bangalore wasn't as challenging as her Hyderabad experience was because this time around she had a manual, a work in progress but useful nevertheless.

Not just apartment hunting but our life in general is a work in progress manual. It's the era of technology and from our Social media websites to our bank applications, it's all intuitive. But living a conscious life always helps. Learning from your own past experiences is more important than having someone play a tutorial for you based on their understanding of life. A beautiful hike for an unfit person could be torture, whereas for a healthy person, it might be the most beautiful experience. Fitness does depend on life choices, but it also depends on the level of privilege to be able to accommodate these choices. A healthy lifestyle does help, but our genes also play a strong role. Either way, our own experience is the only way to know what's best for us. What others have to offer from their life experiences is a guide on understanding how different humans are. We need to try and consciously imprint as much as we can from our life. Past experiences are content for our manual and intuition is a guiding light.

Within 15 days, Maohi moved into her new apartment, and it wasn't as beautiful, but it felt less cold. She was slowly settling in her new life but she constantly missed her old one. She would travel every alternate weekend to visit Aleb in Hyderabad. The first time she booked herself to Hyderabad from Bangalore, her stomach bubbled with joy and it was a familiar feeling. It was a lot like what she felt when she had first moved to Hyderabad

The girl in a pink bow

and had booked herself to visit Punjab. In that moment, she knew, just like Punjab, Hyderabad would always feel like home. It was a wholesome experience for Maohi because she was hopeful that her new city would eventually be as comforting as her previous one. Every weekend that she travelled, she had a skip in her walk and her heart danced with joy. The dullness post returning would be equally upsetting. Though her boyfriend would visit her too, it wasn't as frequent as her visits. She missed her old life as much as she missed Aleb. She missed the clubs she went dancing with her flatmates on ladies' night. She missed the art classes that she took and the bakery she went to post her classes to unwind and read while she sipped her coffee and indulged in her favourite strawberry jar pudding. She had a routine in Hyderabad. Her evenings were spent on the balcony, playing music and hosting guests. On weekends, Maohi had activities like yoga classes or painting classes during the day, and she danced her heart away during the nights. Hyderabad has a lot of cute cafes to grab a coffee and read. She had a favourite cafe for every season - for winters, she wanted to sit in the sun; for monsoons, she wanted something cozy and bright but indoors; for summers, she preferred breezy outdoors with enough shade. She had one for every season and they changed every year.

Maohi's balcony in Bangalore was lonely and her flatmate was fairly irritating. The cafes she visited to read didn't feel bright. She eventually got super busy with work and her colleagues became her life, during and after work. She didn't have anyone to take her out dancing and since she had Aleb back in Hyderabad, there was no chance of having a romantic

The girl in a pink bow

interest that would take her out on dates. Her work became her life and the line between personal and professional started to blur. For once, she had met people she enjoyed working with, the zeal and the spark that she found in Bangalore in her professional life was something that she had never experienced.

Chapter- 5

Maohi went out drinking with her colleagues to her favourite brewery, which was 500 metres from her apartment. There was a long weekend ahead and her team had decided to get a few drinks to commence the long weekend. Maohi didn't have any travelling plans this weekend because she was expected to fulfil some professional obligation of a client. There was a spill-over for which she had to be in the city because there was a possibility that she might have to go meet her client in person if the issue wasn't resolved by her team. She was more than a couple of beers down when she found out that she wouldn't be needed over the weekend. She called Aleb and told him that she had booked herself to travel to Hyderabad. Since it was a last-minute plan, she found the worst possible seat on the bus.

Maohi would take an overnight sleeper bus to travel to Hyderabad. Getting to Bangalore airport from her side of the city wasn't possible post-work. She was bound to miss her flight because she had to either cross Indiranagar or the Bellandur Signal during office hours. Maohi generally finished her work around 7-8 PM. It would take her not less than 4-5 hours to get to the airport to catch a 1-2 AM flight only to land in Hyderabad around 3 AM and get out of the airport by 4 AM and then again take 1 hour from Hyderabad Airport to Aleb's. It was almost a 10-hour ordeal without any sleep. Post work, it was almost impossible for Maohi to be taking up something this challenging, only for the sake of a flight. Sleeper buses took the same time, but she could be sleeping throughout those 10 hours. She anyway hated flying, aeroplanes gave her anxiety. The bus would pick her up from right in front of her office and drop her 10 minutes away from her boyfriend's house.

She had a friend drop her at the pickup spot closest to the brewery and she boarded her bus at 9 PM. She got the last recliner and not the sleeper. The next 10 hours of her life were the bounciest. Maohi felt her spine reaching out to her, all confused, and asking if they were on a mission to save lives because only that would explain this torture. But her liver communicated to her spine that it's the result of it being overworked in the last 2 hours that had led to this decision making. Maohi knew she was guided by her heart to make these mistakes, but it was a little too rash to be boarding a bus just with her laptop bag and not a penny in her wallet. Though Maohi had some cash on her when she was out and about on such journeys, in day-to-day life, she relied on online transactions. Online transactions were not possible because the convenience stores on the highways didn't accept cards and her phone was dead. Starving and being penniless wasn't even the

The girl in a pink bow

biggest problem. It was the belly full of beer and the bumps on the road which didn't make her bladder's life any easier. She avoided using any of the public restrooms in her life, and she had to use the dirtiest of them all on this adventure. She didn't catch any sleep and crashed in her room as soon as she reached Aleb's.

It turned out to be an eventful weekend because all her friends were in town and since it was a long weekend, they were all available to meet. But Aleb was very upset with her stupidity and she realised that it was foolish to do such a thing. Since their relationship was not going in the right direction anyway, she knew it was time to move on. As soon as she boarded her bus back to Bangalore, she knew that it was one of the last few times she would be visiting Hyderabad. She was sad about leaving her life in Hyderabad but there was a different settling feeling to be able to finally do justice to her life in Bangalore and be completely present in her current life. That's when it hit her, that her transformation of feeling at home in Bangalore had begun and even though her heart was heavy, there was a sense of accomplishment and anticipation.

With every mile that she moved away from Hyderabad and closer to Bangalore, she felt liberation vibrating through her body, though Maohi knew that moving on wasn't going to be a straight path and she would keep boomeranging, but she knew she had commenced her journey. She plugged in her earphones and started listening to Green Day as she stared out of her window. She slowly drifted away to sleep.

The girl in a pink bow

Maohi woke up to the sun shining in her eyes as she hadn't closed the curtains; she saw the city and Banaglore started to feel more familiar than it ever had.

Maohi took a cab back home, still hungover by all the intense decision-making. Her heart was heavy as she recollected the emotions of the previous day, but there was an unnecessary smile on her face, which somehow felt in sync with her body. She reached back home, made her favourite coffee in her favourite mug and drank it sitting on her balcony. The balcony was quiet, but it wasn't lonely; it was peaceful. For the past couple of months, Maohi had been escaping her reality and only living in the past. The only time she felt at ease was when she would be in Hyderabad.

When Maohi was 10, her parents started constructing a new home that was around 5 miles from her old home. She was born and brought up in the neighbourhood that she had to leave. The day she moved, she was too young to comprehend her feelings, but her eyes were filled with tears; she couldn't process what she was feeling. When she moved to her new house, her mother would take her back every evening so she could be in her old house. Her parents had sold the house to her mother's sister. Maohi could visit it anytime she wanted and she visited it every day for almost 4 months.

Slowly, she started to make new friends in the neighbourhood of her new house. She was too young to identify the transition she was going through. She was learning to move on from a place that she didn't belong to anymore and learning to adapt to her new surroundings. 15 years later, sitting in the balcony and sipping her coffee, Maohi felt the same emotions and she saw her 10 year self sitting next to her and smiling at her with pride.

Our emotions as we grow do not change; we feel what we felt when we were babies, but we learn to handle them. Rejecting change comes naturally, even if the change is for the good. It's always debatable what is good because just like when Maohi was 10 and she would reject a house 4 times bigger than her previous house, at the age of 25, she wanted to reject a better salary and position for the sake of familiarity. Though monetary benefits could be a driving source to initiate change, how do we gauge an estimate that would be worth trading for comfort and familiarity? The more comfortable you get with your life, the harder it gets to push yourself to grow or progress. On most days, you need an external force creating some disruptions in your life to make the transitions feel easier than the status quo.

When Maohi asked her 10-year-old self when would it be time for her to rest and choose ease and joy over progress and hustle, she only saw a confused 10-year-old looking back at her. Maohi shut her eyes and answered herself that maybe this wasn't her eternal ease and joy, but she was going to let herself get comfortable for a while.

She took a long, hot shower and booked herself on a flight to Bali. Visa on arrival and budget were 2 of her major constraints.

Chapter - 6

Maohi landed in Bali at 9:20 AM. Since it was a last-minute booking, she got a 19-hour flight with an 11-hour layover in Singapore airport. She didn't mind the journey because she loved that airport. She caught a nap on her flight from Singapore to Bali.

Maohi checked into the hotel at 12 noon. It was a small tropical paradise. There were spas and jacuzzis and massages and pools. Perfect for warming a recovering heart. Maohi went for an afternoon massage and was asked to strip down completely and wrap her body in a cotton towel. Maohi had been so consumed with all the things happening in her life that she hadn't stopped to notice her naked body. When she looked at herself in the mirror, she felt her body had lost all the charm and life that it once had. There was nothing wrong but keeping up with work and not resting on weekends so she could travel had tired her. She stretched her body on the massage table and a soft-spoken woman came to ask for her oil preferences.

"Would you prefer Coconut massage oil or shall I use my favourite - Rose Geranium Massage Oil?". Maohi replied, "Coconut Oil. I will come again tomorrow and you can use the other one"."We have vanilla and Piña Colada candles." The lady pointed towards 2 cream candles. "Vanilla, please!". The masseuse lit the candle and dimmed the light.

Though Maohi and Aleb had been having sex occasionally, it had become more of a chore. Aleb felt guilty about talking to another girl, so he hadn't touched Maohi in 3 months now. The warmth and touch of another human on her body was very soothing. It's said that we need 12 hugs daily and Maohi couldn't recollect being hugged 12 times in the entire month. The lady oiled her back and started massaging her, she moved from her back to her hips and then her thighs. Maohi could feel her body rejuvenating as she could feel the blood flow in her system and sense her pale body turning pink. Then, the lady asked Maohi to turn around and bare her front. Maohi did as instructed. The lady started from her legs this time and worked her way to Maohi's breasts. She made sure that every inch of Maohi's body was nicely oiled as she could sense the fatigue. It took her 2 hours to finish her massage. Maohi quickly dressed up as she wanted to grab her lunch, which was going to close at 3 PM and it was already 2:35 PM.

Maohi entered the buffet section, it was a beautiful spread. She ate lobster and prawns with bread and a cheese garlic dip and ordered a glass of chardonnay. Maohi was smiling to herself and her heart was blooming as she enjoyed herself. She was exhausted and ready for a nap. She reached her room and got rid of her clothes. She put out her satin co ord set to change

The girl in a pink bow

into after a warm bath. She filled the tub with warm water and added a few bath salts. She stepped into her tub and poured herself another glass of white. Maohi shut her eyes and threw her head back for 5 minutes and then she took the last sip of her glass and stepped out of the tub. She had no energy to put her satin on, so she just jumped naked into her bed and the white cotton sheets felt what clouds might feel like against her body.

Maohi woke up at around 7 PM in the evening. She despised waking up at this hour. There was something very unsettling about waking up just after twilight, it made her feel blue. She walked to her window and saw how pretty the pool was looking and the staff was lighting the candles on the poolside tables. She turned on the TV and started watching F.R.I.E.N.D.S. Maohi turned on the lights to unpack. There are times when you get this odd feeling that you are being watched, and Maohi starts to feel it. She looked up from her suitcase only to realise that she had turned on the light without drawing her curtains and she was still stark naked. She looked up and saw a man in white staring at her from the room across her window. He was looking at her in amusement and laughed and smirked as she looked up. She blushed and her cheeks turned peachy as she struggled to cover herself with whatever she laid her hands on in the suitcase and slowly closed the drapes. She giggled to herself and felt embarrassed and maybe a little naughty.

Maohi changed into her swimwear that flaunted her curves. She wore a white monokini. The metal rings on her obliques and at the apex of her cleavage held the fabric together. The cold metal against her body was soothing. She put on a cotton dress to walk to the pool.

She started to swim to warm herself up. The pool had another couple and 2 children swimming. It was already 8 PM and the pool closed around 9. Maohi loved to swim and it was one of her favourite workouts. She swam continuously for about 45 minutes when she heard the lifeguard whistle to indicate that she would have to step out in the next 15 minutes. The moment she looked away from the lifeguard, she found herself standing next to a very handsome and a familiar face. It was one of her old flames.

Maohi had been using dating apps since she moved to Hyderabad. Before she found Aleb, she had been going out on dates with people that she met on dating apps. But she never really found any luck on any of these apps. She would get disappointed and switch back to other social media like Facebook or Instagram for mindless scrolling. One day, she saw a friend request from her childhood friend, Karan. Karan used to live in her neighbourhood, and he was her first crush. They rode in the same school bus for about a year and then one day, he disappeared. He was her childhood love and it was pre social media. She had no clue where he had disappeared. 3 years later, she ran into him at one of their neighbourhood parks. They exchanged a brief interaction. Maohi felt that she had passed out during their conversation. She couldn't remember anything and felt dizzy.

Karan was a naughty kid, so his parents had put him into a boarding school in Himachal. He had come back now because his parents wanted him to be in the city for his high school.

Though Karan and Maohi were no longer in the same school, they grew closer after he got back. He was Maohi's first boyfriend. After a year of puppy love, she found out that he had been romancing another girl. Maohi was heartbroken and cut off all ties with him forever.

He reappeared in her life somehow. He was doing law and was based out of Delhi. Maohi's Facebook had "Hyderabad " updated as her city. Karan was due to move to Hyderabad for a month for a case that he had been handling. They reconnected and started to chat. Speaking to him felt like home and she looked forward to going back home after a long day at work and talking to him. Their conversations would fizzle out but they would get back in touch again; this continued for almost a year.

Maohi and Aleb had started off their relationship very casually as she was still healing from a heartbreak and wasn't ready to jump into another relationship. They were in an open relationship for the first 6 months. Eventually, she got seriously involved with Aleb and Karan's relocation kept getting delayed. Though they stayed in touch and Maohi helped Karan find an apartment 50 Mtrs away from her's, within the same complex, she had already started to feel very strongly for Aleb. She eventually told Karan that she was seeing someone else. Their romance had died down a while back and eventually, their friendship also fizzled.

Now Karan's dreamy eyes were staring down at her in the pool. He was looking better than ever. There was water dripping from his hair on his chest and he was smiling at her with a glimmer in his eyes. Maohi was probably unnecessarily exaggerating the look and maybe his eyes were just reflecting

The girl in a pink bow

the candle lights from the tables around them. But Maohi wanted to feel this moment at its highest capacity, so she let herself have it. Maohi hugged Karan and her eyes teared up a little. She held onto the hug a little longer to compensate for her 12 hugs and he took her in his embrace with equal compassion. Karan always made her laugh and he again came up with something witty as soon as she let him go. He knew she was getting emotional and he wanted to ease her. Maohi always laughed with her heart and she never concealed it; it wasn't very lady-like but her laughter was always heartwarming. She laughed with her heart full, wet eyes and an emotional wheeze.

They picked up from where they had left off, there was no awkwardness of any sort. He asked her to join him for dinner and they both wiped their bodies in the candle light. She quickly slipped into her cotton dress. It was a short black dress that knotted at the back, the ribbons tightened right under her swollen breasts. Though she dried herself, her swimwear had collected enough water to imprint on the dress. Karan and Maohi ordered a bottle of wine from the bar next to the pool. Maohi was thirsty, so she gulped her wine down. The drink let her nerves relax from whatever was making her edgy. They drank and spoke about their times from when he was in Delhi and she used to eagerly wait for him to move to Hyderabad.

When Maohi was working as a software consultant in Hyderabad, she was given a below-average quarterly review. Maohi was heartbroken because of the results of her review. She came back home feeling upset and was ignoring Karan's calls that evening. Maohi narrated what happened on a text and explained why she wasn't in the mood for a conversation. She was doubting her self-worth and didn't have the energy to entertain anyone. She got up to get some fresh air and on her way out, she saw her reflection in the glass of her sliding door that opened into the balcony. Her face had turned pale and her eyes were dark.

The negative emotions inside of us reflect on our faces. We can tell by looking at people how their day is going. If we see that their faces are glowing, it's mostly because their body and mind are in sync and are fit. The quality of blood circulating through our body is an indication of our physical fitness and the quality of thoughts circulating through our body is an indication of our mental fitness. Consuming and festering negative thoughts or emotions deteriorates our mental health. Poor mental health impacts our physical health and we start to feel physically sick. Mental and Physical health always sync up; that is why it's very important to focus on the fitness of body and mind alike. If we work on our mental health and have a strong mind, then on days of physical illness, we can rely on a strong mental health and vice versa.

Maohi's working hours and erratic food habits kept her from focusing on her physical health and mental health wasn't something that was under her purview at the moment; she was ignorant of its importance, to say the least. She stood on the balcony and lit a cigarette that had been lying there from the previous night. She smoked to calm her nerves and started to analyse her life. She went deep into her thoughts and was brought back to reality by the sound of notifications. She took her last drag and picked her body up. She could feel her heart was heavy and she could physically feel the weight of having to

The girl in a pink bow

manoeuvre herself from one position to another. She opened her phone to find a list of screenshots of appreciation emails sent to her from her first ever project as a consultant. Karan had saved the screenshots Maohi had sent him months ago from when she had received the appreciation emails from her seniors for successfully completing her first project. Maohi had fallen on her knees and tears flooded her eyes. In one moment, he had changed the emotions going through her body. Not only were those emails proof of her self-worth but the fact that Karan went that extra mile to help her feel better was overwhelming. She called him back and wept on the phone while thanking him. That is when Karan told her that he'd be moving to Hyderabad in 3 months. 3 months turned into a year.

Now, running into him in Bali was a pleasant welcome. It started to rain, and Karan and Maohi had to move indoors. They decided to have another bottle of wine but the restaurant in the hotel was almost closing down. So they decided to take the bottle to Karan's room and order room service. Maohi absentmindedly followed him to his room and sat on the chair. She asked him about the duration of his stay. Karan had booked for 2 nights, and he had to fly out after 2 days. He poured them both a glass each and played some music. Karan spoke about his work and the places he had travelled. He always wanted to be a lawyer, and though the job was very demanding and almost a torture to his circadian rhythm, it was fulfilling. Maohi hoped to find the passion that Karan's eyes emitted when he spoke about his favourite closing arguments. He loved flying out to one of the tropical destinations after winning an important case. Karan told her about how excited he was when

The girl in a pink bow

he won his life's first major case. In that moment, Maohi imagined what it would feel like if she travelled by his side to these tropical destinations to celebrate his wins. Maohi had been nodding and smiling as he spoke. Karan noticed her smile immediately fall right before she took her sip. He asked her if he was speaking too much about himself and if it was bothering her. The fabric of that question was ingenuity because he had noticed since he saw her at the pool that her smile wouldn't touch her eyes, and he knew it wasn't his stories. She felt at peace but it was numbing and not wholesome. She just told him that a lot had happened since they last met; she wasn't willing to go into any details, and he didn't want to push her.

He asked Maohi if she wanted to step out on the balcony to get some fresh air, and she agreed to it. She noticed that she was on the same floor as her own room. Then it hit her that her room was right across from Karan's and the man looking at her while she was engrossed in her suitcase was him. She turned to face him and she saw the same smirk. Maohi blushed but pretended to cover it under her rage. She got furious and asked him, "What kind of a pervert peeps into the hotel rooms of other people?". He started laughing and asked her, "What sort of an exhibitionist entertains half heartedly?". Her face turned into a darker shade of red and she turned to walk away from him.

He held her from her waist and pulled her closer to his body in an attempt to keep her from walking away. He softly apologised into her ears. He told her that when he was checking-in in the afternoon, he thought he had seen her rushing towards the restaurant from the spa. Karan had asked the concierge checking him in that he was to meet Ms. Maohi at the hotel and to check if she had checked in. The concierge had told him that she had, and he requested a room on the same floor. He told Karan that the room was available on the same floor but on the opposite end. The building was in a semi-circle, so their windows were facing each other. Karan told her that he had walked all the way to her room this afternoon and was about to knock. He decided otherwise. " I was hoping to run into you eventually, but" he paused "I didnt want to impose". Maohi figured that he thought that she could have been on a holliday with Aleb, and so he didn't knock. She remembered that she was bathing around the time Karan would have been at her door. The thought of what would have happened had he actually knocked and she had let him in sent electricity down her spine. Karan told her that he was only trying to make sure Maohi was all by herself or if she had company. His intentions were not to look at her naked body. He accepted that though he was inquisitive is why he was looking into her window, but once he saw what he saw, he did not want to look away. He accepted honestly and shamelessly. "I am not going to lie, I didn't even want to make an attempt to look away and it irritated me when you closed your curtains."

Chapter - 7

Maohi's breathing started to get rattled and Karan could see the rise and drop of her breasts. He loosened his grip but didn't let go. He was worried she would bolt but Maohi stayed safely fastened. She had finally found her shell to collapse into and be in her femininity. She tilted her head backwards and rested it on his chest. Karan knew she was comfortable but he didn't want to push it. He let her stand there and tightened his grip again to make sure she felt secure. He kissed her forehead and took her indoors. Karan poured them both another glass of wine. He told Maohi that he had been aching to kiss her full lips. He looked at her and he told her that he was going to kiss her and if she wanted to stop him she had 2 seconds to say so. He grabbed her from her waist and settled his hand behind her head, tangling his fingers in her hair. Looked dead into her eyes, smiled and said, "Time up, love!". They kissed.

The girl in a pink bow

Karan had switched on the TV when they entered and scrolled through the menu until Maohi jumped when she saw Harry Potter on the list. Harry Potter was still playing on the TV. Maohi told him that Harry Potter was the only fantasy that she ever wanted to be a part of but at this moment, she wouldn't trade her fantasy like reality even for a letter from Hogwarts. Karan laughed as he planted a kiss on her forehead.

After cleaning up, He gave Maohi his favourite t-shirt and they got into bed. Karan started to discuss the menu to order in. They both settled on Pasta and Ginger ale to go with. Maohi jumped out of the bed to make herself some coffee. Then she tucked herself back in to watch Harry Potter while she munched on a cookie with her hot beverage. Karan was checking his emails. He generally went through his work emails before booking a spa appointment to ensure that his relaxation did not overlap with any scheduled meetings. He had checked into this hotel for the spas that they offered.

Housekeeping knocked on the door and delivered their meal. They ate their dinner while Voldemort tried to kill Harry Potter.

Every moment of romance that you share with any partner is like a small love story within itself. There are partners who get together purely for the pleasure of exchanging bodily fluids but Maohi never believed in that. She knew her every romantic encounter could not be her forever love. But she always enjoyed her romantic escapades as if they were whole in themself, like a fairytale that was only hers to read. On occasions, she would share a chapter or two with others but only she knew the totality and extent of it. She lived a multitude of such love stories,

The girl in a pink bow

though they all began with the hope of an everlasting love but unfortunately, they all came with an expiration date. Maohi was optimistic about finding her forever love and most of her fairy tale romances had enough potential. Every heartbreak left a bitter taste in her mouth but her enthusiasm to experience love wouldn't diminish.

It was a bright, sunny morning. Maohi and Karan took a long bath. Karan soaped Maohi's body like a boy cleans his most prized possession. They stood under the shower, hugging each other for what felt like an eternity. They both knew the chances of a successful relationship were bleak.

The 21st century isn't the best time for people wanting to prioritise their personal life in their 20s. Professional life takes a heavy toll and long distances are exasperating. They stepped out from the shower with an unsaid reassurance that gave the required satisfaction. The skip in Maohi's walk was back and though it was too early for her to feel any butterflies, she definitely felt some tingling and that was enough. She walked to her room to put on something a little more appropriate for the breakfast table.

Chapter-8

Maohi walked through the palm trees that led to the hotel's private beach. She hadn't had the chance to be on the beach yet. The moment her feet touched the sand, her hands automatically started to undress her until she was in nothing but her cute, turquoise seashell bikini. The water glittered like diamonds under the sun. She kept her clothes on a sunbed and she walked towards the ocean. She swam in the cold, calm and clear blue water. She felt free and rejuvenated and she promised herself to never let anything interfere with the joys of life that she was fortunate enough to experience. Maohi was empty stomach and drained from all the love making. Salt water wasn't making her dehydration any better. She decided to get herself a lot of water and some coffee with sugary treats.

As Maohi walked towards her clothes, she saw Karan sitting on the sunbed, sipping his coffee. He told her that he had booked a couples massage and spa in the afternoon for the two of them. They enjoyed the lavish spread of breakfast by the

The girl in a pink bow

beach and went back to Maohi's room for a nap. They cuddled and spoke about their aspirations in life and things that drove them.

There are a few of us who aspire for the stars, but the fear of ridicule keeps us from expressing our desires. They gave each other the podium and a safe space to talk out loud about their unreasonable dreams. Maohi spoke about how she one day wanted to own a little bakery and a bed and breakfast on a white sand beach. She wanted to spend her mornings swimming in the ocean and afternoons writing. She spoke of her dreams with a fascination that brought a twinkle in her eyes.

She described, "The entire bakery would be painted in white, with the edges painted in turquoise. The wooden furniture in the bakery would be painted turquoise with an earthy finish. The bakery would have 3 tables for two and a bookshelf indoors. The counter would have a wooden window that opens out front like a tiny window shutter and becomes a sort of standing table for people to place orders from outside. There will be 2 two-seater tables outdoors in the front. The frame of the order window and entrance would be covered with a red grapevine that would extend to the roof and cover the railings on the section of the roof that faces the front. The other side of the bakery would be a glass wall, facing the ocean. 3 outdoor 2 seater tables would be adjacent to the glass wall, and a small stall of fresh flowers would be at the back. The bakery would have a new menu of not more than 6 dishes, curated every morning. The aroma of butter, vanilla and chocolate would always surround the bakery. There would be a Persian cat sitting on the counter, trying to push the coins off the slab.

I will wake up at 7 AM and do yoga on the beach, and then I will take a dip in the ocean to cool down. Post-workout, I would have a buttery protein with bread and a cup of Americano on the side. Then, I would open my bakery around 10 AM to entertain my guests and read till noon and then go take a nap. I will wake up again at 3 PM to go take a dip in the ocean and then come back and write in the room above the bakery." She wanted a 3 bedroom set above her bakery. All 3 bedrooms with big glass walls that open onto balconies. She continued, "The glass walls of the rooms would have white lacy curtains, and the frames of all 3 rooms and their balconies would have the same red grapevine. The balconies will have hammocks and a wooden turquoise staircase that leads to the beach through the flower stall. I will have 1 room to myself and the other 2 to be listed on Airbnb. Post Sunset, I would change into a cute evening dress to host my customers and interact with the travellers." She oscillated between the idea of having a partner or choosing to be by herself. There were days she imagined passionate lovemaking on the balcony, and then there were days she preferred to read/write in solitude. Though she wanted love in her life, she wasn't sure if the love that she was looking for existed at all in this century.

Karan heard Maohi speak about her dreams with such passion and enthusiasm that it was almost contagious. He could almost imagine himself coming to Maohi's bakery post his important wins. Maohi's lips curled into a sheepish smile the moment she snapped out of the vision that she had entered and her eyes met with the reality in her bed.

The girl in a pink bow

They received their call for their spa appointment and Maohi didn't realise that she had been asleep for almost 3 hours. They went in for their massages and spas and ended their pampering by enjoying each other's bodies in the jacuzzi post the spa. Their faces were glowing with rejuvenation and joy. The sun had almost set and they went out to sit by the beach and ordered a bottle of wine. Maohi and Karan ordered a bottle of white and red, respectively. The candles on the tables were lit again and by the time they finished their first glass, it was time for dinner. They ordered a lobster and steak. They walked back to their respective rooms absentmindedly, not sure if this was it or if they should be spending another night together.

Maohi entered her room and saw her satin night suit from the previous day still hanging there. She changed into her night suit and sat on her bed to read. Most of us readers start reading in a socially acceptable posture but after an hour of reading, our bodies are contorted into shapes that make our skeletal systems weep. Maohi had surrendered to one of those postures in her bed when she heard a knock on the door. Karan was standing there with Brownie and Vanilla ice cream dripping with a thick layer of Nutella. He told her that he had called for room service and the aroma of buttery brownie, Chocolatey nutella and vanilla ice cream - reminded him of her bakery and at that moment, he knew that he wanted to spend the rest of the night cuddling, watching movies and eating unhealthy desserts. Maohi smiled and then blushed the moment Karan's gaze landed on what she was reading - "50 Shades of Grey".

They finished their dessert and laughed about random things and ideas for hours with "The Holliday " playing on the

TV in the background. Eventually, they cuddled into the bed to complete the movie and drifted into a deep sleep. Maohi and Karan both had to check out the next morning. They skipped breakfast to sleep in a little longer and then they checked out and kissed each other goodbye. Maohi texted him after boarding her plane back to India.

Maohi: Thank you for everything. I loved our time together.

Karan: I wouldn't have had it any other way.

They had discussed their situation in life. Maohi had to move to North America for her Masters and Karan was too invested in his career at the moment and he would go wherever his work took him. They knew they couldn't be involved romantically, at least not in the foreseeable future. They had decided to "stay in touch"

Chapter - 9

Maohi got called into her boss's office and he told her that her performance was not up to the mark. She had seen it coming, adjusting into the new city and a freshly wounded heart were keeping her from giving her best at work. The same evening, her team was off to a brewery in Bangalore for a couple of beers. Maohi was feeling low but she went along anyway. She knew that if she didn't perform, she would lose her job and she didn't want that. She sulked, sitting behind Mahim as they rode from their office towards their evening shenanigans. Maohi had found herself something close to a family with her colleagues. Her closest friend in Bangalore shared her name with Maohi's closest friend and flatmate in Hyderabad, Shien. Mahim, Shien, Shahid, Rudra and Ruham were Maohi's little family in Bangalore. The team was led by Sir Panesaar, who had now given Maohi critical feedback about her performance. Maohi and Mahim were extremely fond of each other and confided in each other. They got along really well and understood each other to the point that they could complete each other's sentences. She told Mahim about her ultimatum.

Bangalore is a big city and the traffic makes it even bigger. If you have a friend who volunteers to drop you off at the airport, the chances of you landing at your destination before he reaches back home are significantly higher. Most people watched the Game Of Thrones new episode releases in cabs, on their way to work. For the sake of operational feasibility, the entire team was spread out to different locations within the city. However, the entire team got together every Friday to discuss progress and issues. That's when Maohi went out with all her colleagues every Friday and they drank like they had a liver on standby. The next morning, all of them had swollen eyes from the lack of sleep and a heavy head with a hangover. No matter how many times they promised themselves to never repeat it again, every single time the time spent was worth the exasperation on the following day.

Maohi got extremely attached to Mahim and Shien during this process. Maohi, Mahim and Shien were all based out of the same location and lived barely a km apart. Maohi struggled with her first flatmate as they quarrelled over petty issues like "where to dry their clothes". When her flatmate finally moved out, she gave the room to 2 sisters without Maohi's consent. Maohi wasn't happy about the entire situation but she never had the energy to fight it out because she was overcompensating for lagging behind at work in the last few months. These 2 new girls moved in, they never really lived there. Though they would timely transfer their rent to the owner, there was no sign of them ever being in the flat. Their room was always locked and

The girl in a pink bow

the thought of what might be inside the room frightened Maohi on most nights. The balcony of her room was connected to the main balcony of the living area and these girls had access to the house. Not just them but their friends, who came with them on their moving day, had access to the house and Maohi's room. The balcony door didn't lock. Maohi never slept in peace as she knew that random strangers had access to her room, though it was a gated society but the lease deed had the names of the girls and these girls, whom Maohi had no clue about, had access to her room. Living alone in a big and fairly new city and knowing that random people have access to your room at any point in the day and night kept Maohi on her toes and anxious when she was at home.

The only time Maohi felt at peace was when she could spend the night at Mahim or Shien's. Those were the only nights she felt safe and got some goodnight's sleep. However, she couldn't impose that all the time because Mahim had other flatmates that were not comfortable with a girl staying over and Shien had a boyfriend. Yet they both accommodated Maohi on days she had no energy to keep her guard up all night and would decide to crash at either of their places. Since Maohi was working 6 days a week and almost every weekend was spent at a friend's place, there were multiple times when she came home to a house that had no electricity. The electricity bill would never reach Maohi due to her unavailability. She kept requesting her gatekeepers to slide the bill from under her apartment door. Even after agreeing to this arrangement, Maohi never came home to a bill on the floor. Which led the Electricity department to disconnect her power often. One night, Maohi came in really late to her apartment to find out that the electricity was disconnected, again! Neither did she have any energy nor was there anyone around to resolve the issue, even if she immediately paid her bill. She, however, paid her bill in hopes of waking up to a functional house. She used her phone's torch to find herself some candles and lit them. She took a candlelight bath and ordered some food. Luckily, there was enough hot water to refresh her. She stepped out of a wholesome shower and draped herself in a soft pink cotton towel. She tied up her hair and put on her bunny ear hairband to do her skincare. Maohi's phone rang and she instructed the delivery agent to leave the food at her doorstep because there wasn't enough light to go digging for fresh clothes from the cupboard. She put her ear against her apartment door to make sure she heard the delivery agent drop her food and get onto the elevator. Maohi opened her door only after she heard the elevator door close. As soon as she opened her door to collect her food, she saw her next door neighbour struggling with his keys to open the apartment. The elevator that took her delivery agent to the ground floor was also the same elevator that brought her neighbour to the 7th floor. He was struggling to open the door because he was carrying multiple grocery bags. Without looking at Maohi, he asked her if she could help him with the lock because of the bags. "Could you please just hold this for a second?". When he didn't hear her respond, he looked up to find her staring at him in her towel, wide-eyed, embarrassed and apologetic for not being able to help him because she wasn't appropriately dressed. He laughed and smiled when he saw her standing at the door of a blacked-out apartment with a few candles. Tushar could tell that she had

The girl in a pink bow

just stepped out of her shower; he wondered if he was smelling her shower gel or if it were the candles. He politely muttered, "Never mind! Looks like you could use some help instead," and got back to his struggle with the apartment lock.

Maohi got back inside and locked her door immediately. She sat down on her bed and was grateful to find that her laptop was at 69%. She played "Desperate Housewives" while she ate her Ramen. She drifted off to sleep. Maohi woke up to a click of the door, she thought that the girls were entering the apartment. She could hear whispers but couldn't make out how many people were talking. She lifted her head to hear more closely, only to find a man staring back at her from her balcony, and the click she heard was from her balcony door and not from the living area. She screamed in the hopes of waking up the neighbour she saw earlier that night. The only person she woke up from her scream was herself. Maohi had been dreaming about what she dreaded almost every night. Her nightmare woke her up and she was drenched in sweat. It was post dawn and her electricity was back. While Maohi waited for her water to warm up, she updated her electricity bill payment to autopay.

Maohi had stopped visiting Hyderabad and focused all her energy on her work. She trained her team and revamped the working strategy, she hired a few more people for her team and started to work towards becoming the best Team. Maohi's team had a very close bond; she was personally present for all her team members in any way they needed assistance in order to perform well. She had an assistant, Sarang. Sarang managed most of her important work and covered for her. She had managed to set up a good team that worked hard and reaped results of their hard work.

Maohi was handed over a team that was absolutely demotivated. Even after all day's work, their efforts were not appreciated either due to system limitations that were not highlighted to the superiors or due to lack of visibility. Maohi fixed these issues and ensured that every team member had the confidence to pull off their style of work and none of them ever hesitated to reach out to the senior management whenever they felt they were wronged. Maohi empowered her team so they were ambitious and hard working. She assured them their laurels as and when due.

Maohi had been applying to various B Schools to pursue an MBA. One of the Schools that called her back was based in Hyderabad as well. She wasn't aware of their Hyderabad campus; she thought that they only had one campus in Toronto and that the Hyderabad campus was just an official building. After the first round of her online interview, she got a call for an in-person interview. After months again now, Maohi had decided to get onto her "once a regular route". Post her work, she boarded her bus to Hyderabad.

Chapter - 10

Maohi went back to her old apartment, she was going to stay with Shien (Hyderabad) this time. She was in touch with Aleb and he knew of her progress. Aleb knew that she was going to be in the city only for a day. Maohi reached Hyderabad and went for her interview in the evening. During her interview, she was asked about her priority for the campus. The program had 2 options: 1) 1st 8 months in Hyderabad and next 1 year in Toronto or 2) Entire course in Toronto. Maohi had decided to relocate and move out of India for at least the next 5 years, so she thought that she would preferably spend as much time in India, close to her family, as she could before she relocated. She was assured that the quality of education would be the same because the professors would fly in from the main campus for the lectures. Though this meant that it would limit her exposure, she thought that the initial months would be about getting to know her batchmates and that eventually, she would get the relevant exposure and the interaction that she wanted. At least, that's what she thought.

Maohi had her admit in her mailbox within 1 hour of arriving back at Kay Towers. She was excited about getting through, and a part of her stupid, hopeless romantic self thought that it was the universe bringing her and Aleb together once again. She had her bus booked for the same night. She met Aleb for a few drinks to celebrate her admittance and when they were waiting at her bus stop, she told him that if he wanted, she was willing to miss her bus that night. Aleb hesitated at first, but as he saw the bus enter the departure point, he started to drive away with Maohi in the car.

Maohi called her manager and told him that she would have to stay back another day for some formalities, but her manager was pushing her to be back. The next day was the entire Bangalore team's review. A part of Maohi thought that she was getting fired and that was the reason that Sir Panesar was pushing for her to be in the office as he needed to do it in person. If Maohi isn't there, the word would get out anyway and the conversation post that would be uncomfortable. Instead, her manager gave her the news that her zone was the best zone of the previous month and that she and her team were to receive an award during the review. Maohi jumped with excitement and she felt that all that was going wrong had suddenly changed directions and things were just going to work out for her.

They went home and celebrated, both her admit and the best team award. She discussed what it was going to be like going forward. Maohi could tell that Aleb was having a change of heart and he was considering spending the rest of his life with

The girl in a pink bow

Maohi, even if it meant disappointing his mother. They were holding hands and Aleb was closing in; she could sense sexual intimacy radiating between their bodies. They started to kiss passionately, but before Aleb could undress her, Maohi blurted out about being with Karan. Aleb stopped and walked out of the room immediately.

Aleb had gone holidaying to the States with the girl he was supposed to get married to, but somehow Maohi's 2 days with Karan were unacceptable. Maohi followed him and told him that it was a result of wanting to move on and being opportunistic about having a chance to do so. She tried to explain it to him but he just wouldn't listen. They slept in different rooms that night. Maohi kept pondering upon "whatever happens, happens for the good" and something conflicting to it "Checks and balances".

We fall in love knowing that it can be painful, but we hope for the best. Maybe "wishful thinking" is our enemy. All the lovers that we take in a lifetime have a part of us that belongs to them and part of theirs that belongs to us. Both these pieces freeze somewhere in time that was shared between the two. Any memory from that phase is triggered through an external factor like a song, a fragrance, etc., and we go back in time. Though there are days when we go back to that time and it feels so relevant and warm and comforting but then there are also days when it feels like an alien world and something that happened in a different lifetime. What we feel depends on our frame of mind in the present.

We all hope for a fairytale ending even though a part of us knows that they don't exist. The problem is the "checks and balances" that nature puts in place and whenever there is something too good to be true, it probably isn't true. The conundrum lies in the absolute anxiety of a blissful phase, knowing that it wouldn't last. People are too worried about things going well, knowing that a dreadful "balance" is just around the corner. The dilemma is - whether to feel so deeply the joy in that moment or pace it in order to minimise the eventual pain? To be Extreme or to be Reined?

Aleb dropped Maohi off at Kay Towers in the morning. Maohi had apologised in length the night before but she felt silly about it because Aleb had moved on and was holidaying with another girl. No part of him showed any remorse for his decisions. She felt as if he was passively conveying his thoughts on promiscuity in women vs promiscuity in men.

Maohi was pro-choice kind of feminist. She had once had an argument with Rudr about women in corporate. Rudr was of the opinion that women get periods and they can't be as productive as men on those days. He was opposing the idea of "period leaves" once in a month. Maohi's response to that was that women should also be given privileges while factoring cutoff percentages. Women have the same amount of time as men for the preparation, and no extra time is given to factor the days when they aren't performing at their best - courtesy ovaries. Maohi had scored 85%. There are 365 days in a year, and if a woman isn't as competent as a man (for no fault of her own) for 3 days every month, 12 months a year. That's $(36/365)*100 = 9.9\%$. This percentage difference should be factored in while deciding college cut-offs or hiring cut-offs. This argument was relevant if the cut-off, to get to where men and women are competing neck to neck, factored in this 10%. That is, a man with 95% can make such a remark because he is at par with Maohi post-factoring the time she lost in bleeding. But if no such thing is factored then women have achieved their positions next to men with bleeding vaginas, now the next step can't be taken away from them just because they might be incompetent on 3 days a month. If women were given these 3 extra days, a technically equal number of days as men, they might have conquered more.

Maohi wasn't a toxic feminist, but she believed in equality and fairness. No two hearts (men or women) beat differently. They desire, love and hurt equally. Societies normalising infidelity by men is absolutely ridiculous.

She went up to her old apartment. Shien had made her coffee and there were freshly baked muffins in the house. They both had their morning coffee with some muffins and spoke about their dreams, desires and what they wanted to achieve in life. Shien had her own set of issues with her love life, which Maohi and she discussed on and off, but that morning wasn't about their love life but about realising how their love life was just a small part of a wholesome life that they dreamt of. Shien left for work and Maohi went to the mall. Maohi had her eye on a Swarovski band that she kept trying on whenever she went to the Swarovski store. Luckily for her, the same band was available in the Hyderabad store. She had promised to buy herself the ring the minute she felt she had accomplished something significant. The admit and the award were not significant in isolation, but together, they were an achievement worth celebrating with a crystal band around her finger and a chili's burger. Maohi ordered herself a mug of beer to go with her burger and enjoyed her afternoon by herself. She went to her old friends Ankit and Vinek's apartment after her little splurge. They had been a constant support to her throughout, and she felt like celebrating her achievements with them. They drank a couple of beers and ordered good food. She rested at their apartment for a bit, and then they dropped her off at her bus stop. Maohi knew she would be back in Hyderabad within a couple of months and she was excited about starting her new journey.

Is it normal to keep gravitating back to our past? We try to move on from things that aren't meant for us and eventually get to a place where we entertain these memories as sweet nostalgia. People keep saying that happy thoughts and positive energy help us manifest happiness. If we live in the past and in the past we had chosen to just look at the bright side then maybe in nostalgia we only visit happiness. We can only visit our state of mind and not travel back in time, not in one piece at least. How do we find the balance? If the past always feels so sweet, how do we really move on? It feels like a tradeoff between moving on and having a happy life. Only if we see things for what they are can we move on. If we keep seeing the best in it, wouldn't we just stick around for eternity? What is reality anyway? We never have access to the absolute truth. There are assumptions and then understanding of a situation based on past experiences. We have all created our own little realities, and while these might overlap, they are never identical copies; no two people experience the same moment exactly the same way. Our realities are a reflection of who we are, and if we

The girl in a pink bow

understand that, then maybe we would choose happiness more often.

Is life just a canvas of projections?

Subconsciously, we identify and perceive our present as a projection of our past. This blend of past and present existing as a single entity in a hypothetical dimension is manipulated into an experience. Which eventually acts as a wireframe for an ever-evolving art called "LIFE". Throughout our lives we keep broadening our canvas and scrutinise every aspect to be expanded, highlighted or left in the corner to be ignored or repainted.

All shades of our feelings deserve an outlet, we ought to cherish our life under the diverse spectrum. Every moment will have a different colour and each phase will have a dominating shade. But as the phase passes, feelings change, we evolve and wisdom - is the side effect of this change and a byproduct of the experience.

Evolving as a version of ourselves is a lifelong process, which might disrupt harmony in naive relationships. We have to find someone open to embracing our mistakes while we upgrade. Anyone accepting and understanding of this process will always be at least partially, if not completely, enlightened. This enlightenment would be interfering, we shouldn't be afraid of letting people take charge of our paint brush, given that our canvas never ceases to be "US". Take the back seat and enjoy their expression, provided we are aware that the chances to fix a wrong color are limited. We should leave enough room for our own fuck-ups. It's like making our own food we know how we like it BEST, but sometimes GOOD is enough if it's served to us without having to put in the effort. Though it doesn't hurt to hand over our recipe but experiencing something new adds to the charm. All this external interference can either blur our masterpiece with fear or encourage us to appreciate the foreign indulgences.

We should never be afraid to use an alien colour on our canvas. The brain is an immensely powerful tool which amplifies the fear of the *unknown* to a degree x folds beyond the extreme, which might be the reason for our resistance. But we need to experiment. We might find love in the faintest shade of blue. After all, isn't evolving all about breaking the cliches and acknowledging the unknown?

Chapter - 11

Fortunately, Maohi was available for her next 2 awards and eventually won her team the rolling trophy. Her company had a rolling trophy, which was handed over to different winners. Any team that won "best performance" in a city 3 months in a row got to keep it. Maohi bought that trophy home for life. She was super excited to tell all the important people in her life about her achievements. She was confused if Aleb was as important in the present or was he a thing of the past that she had to move on from. She had to start celebrating her life without making him an active participant to actually leave it all behind. She decided not to celebrate this victory with him. Maohi deleted the text she had already typed and opened another text window. The other person that she really wanted to reach out to was "Karan". No one celebrated Maohi like Karan. Karan had compensated for the faith in her, whenever she lost it in herself. Unfortunately, he never became an active part of Maohi's life, at least not active enough to become as important as to share important details of her life. Maohi opened her "Home" WhatsApp group and shared a photo of her trophy and certificate with her parents.

Maohi was so consumed in her life - nursing a wounded heart, outperforming herself at work and getting an admit that she didn't notice when Bangalore started to feel like Home. By the time the seasons started to repeat themselves, it was time for Maohi to put down her papers and uproot again. She couldn't tell if Bangalore grew on her while she was dealing with extremities or if Banaglore accommodated her to help her through a tough one. Maohi moved in with Shien for her last month in the city. She went to all her favorite breweries and cafes to order her beers and coffees, one last time as a local.

One night after work, during Maohi's last weekend in Bangalore. Maohi and Shien decided to go out. They went out to a bar where Maohi saw "Aleb" she stared in his direction only to realise that he was a look alike. Maohi told Shien that she wanted to go tell "the look alike at the bar" that he was really cute. Shien motivated her enough to push every ounce of apprehension out of Maohi's body. Not only did Maohi tell him that he was cute but she also invited him and his friend to their table. 10 minutes into the conversation, she realised that both the boys were as dull as they come. Though the boys wanted to take them club hopping but the girls escaped it.

Maohi and Shien, disappointed by the crowd and the music, eventually came back home and decided to sit on their balcony with some beers and ordered pizzas. They sat there, discussing their romantic escapades in life and how difficult it is to find peace in a relationship. Both agreed that loving relationships are the real unicorns of big city life. They could hear Shien's flatmate enjoying one of her such romantic escapades, so they played some music to fade her.

We keep cribbing about how hard it is to find love in this world, but the real problem is to find and sustain it. How do you sustain love if you are constantly uprooting for your professional growth? It's also almost impossible to progress if you just stay put in one place; only a lucky few get to move forward in their professional life without having to relocate. The world going global and the infinite opportunities to move to infinite locations are probably the real reasons behind why most love stories don't last, or maybe the right ones do.

They both spent the entire night on the balcony and slept in the next day. Just like most weekends in Bangalore. Shien's chef had prepared butter garlic prawns and hot and spicy squid with some oregano and cheddar cheese bread. They woke up and enjoyed their meal as they watched Two and a Half Men. She felt at home but now it was time to move, Again! Maohi experienced a weird exhaustion, the reason behind this exhaustion was knowing that it would at least take her 2 full years to feel at home again because next 1 year she would be in Chandigarh (initially) and then in Hyderabad and it would take her at least 1 full year to settle in in Canada.

Chapter - 12

Maohi's team brought her a gorgeous cake and gifted her a beautiful watch on her last day of work. She bid farewell and sent off her signing-off email. It is always very overwhelming to send off that last email. Corporate life for Maohi was nothing less than a toxic relationship she had had with the men who came into her life. Though they all took more from her than they ever gave, detaching herself from the stability that they brought to her life was a task.

She spent her last night with her Bangalore family for one last time. Maohi had a soft corner for Mahim, she thought he had it too. But they both knew that there was something missing that would always keep them from dating. They settled for being good friends because they respected the bond way too much to let an unsuccessful romance ruin their relationship.

The next day, she woke up and ran to the airport; she barely got any sleep. Maohi wasn't sure if it was dehydration or sleep

The girl in a pink bow

deprivation or just depression that kicks in after the high settles. But Maohi's eyes kept flooding with tears. Hyderabad was just a bus journey away, and she felt that Aleb was always reachable but she knew once she boarded her flight back home, there would be no looking back. She called Aleb and wept throughout her check-in. She asked him if there was any future possible for them, but he succumbed to the family pressure, he had agreed to marry the girl of his mother's liking.

Maohi landed back home and all her tears and heaviness vanished. It had rained that morning in Chandigarh, she felt that god poured on behalf of her for whatever part of her grief was left. She reached home, took a hot water bath, ate her favourite meal and went to sleep. Maohi had a lot of catching up on her sleep to do. Her last week in Bangalore was crazy as she had to meet her friends and colleagues before she left. She also had to pack her life up once again and uproot. Coming back home, before she moved again to Hyderabad to begin her MBA journey, was a much-needed break. She did whatever she had missed doing in the past year and a half. On weekdays, she had her yoga lessons, painting lessons, golfing lessons and swimming. On weekends, she went to her Latin dancing classes. Maohi had missed dancing and she didn't have anyone in Chandigarh to go dancing with. So she ended up taking lessons for a new dance form. Every alternate week, if and when she found time, she went to her favourite bookstore where she went as a child. She would spend hours there to pick out her favourite book. Then, for the next 2 weeks, post her morning yoga lesson, she would go to a cafe and sit and read. Maohi had 2 months to live the life that she had been missing out on.

Most people aren't even sure about what makes them happy. Maohi, on the other hand, had a list of things that she knew brought her joy. Life is very short to experience all the ecstasies that it has to offer which also means that you would be spared a lot of sorrows too. Exploration helps us identify the things that light our soul on fire and discard the ones that aren't for us. We put more weightage on exploring the happiness that might exist somewhere out in the world and draw our attention away from what we already have. We see the perks of most things that are beyond our reach, while the downsides are hidden or sugar-coated. It's like what we experience on social media; almost all users constantly post only about their good days. The Instagram feeds of a newlywed would be flooded with the love she shares with her partner, but you wouldn't see her posting about the insecurities she feels when he carelessly flirts with his old flame. All the single people on her list might end up feeling unfulfilled. Nothing in this entire arrangement would direct them to appreciate their peace of mind. This is just an example of married life but it's true for all events in life. We are brought up around idioms like "All that glitters is not gold", "Grass is always greener on the other side of the fence", etc, yet we forget to apply these learnings. We need to be happy with what we have. It's okay not to be satisfied; only then would you strive for the best. But that journey shouldn't keep us from appreciating the things that we need to be grateful for. It's blissful to find the perfect partner and share your life with someone. It's amazing to be loved and cherished. But the absence of romantic love shouldn't make us desperate. Settling for a life partner out of this desperation can lead to unhappiness. Love is the most common thing that we all are

The girl in a pink bow

looking for. But sometimes a swim with a poolside bar post a morning game of golf could be, if not more, at least, as blissful. If you aren't a swimmer or a golfer, then maybe a cup of coffee with an apple pie and a book with the best romance in the world on a crisp autumn morning after a strenuous session of aerial yoga. If not this, then maybe painting; if not painting, then maybe dancing. These things just take a little effort but are fulfilling. Maybe Bollywood and Hollywood have been selling love for the longest because it's the most common factor and would garner an audience. Love is also the toughest thing to find and sustain. These hobbies, on the other hand, that are personal to us all are easily accessible but not celebrated enough because they are too personal, and any marketing strategy might not make business sense. That is probably the reason why they rarely reach us. How many women would want to dirty/break their nails for pottery, or how many men would not have their masculinity questioned? But then there would be a group of people for whom pottery might be meditation. We need to build a society that glorifies the effort that one takes to identify their happy place from these small yet accessible activities. It's very important to have massive unrealistic dreams but being present in the life that happens outside the pursuit of these dreams brings in the required balance.

For every dream that we aspire to achieve, we would collect at least 10 more bigger dreams in the process. If you have INR 1,00,000 you might aspire to earn enough to procure a Dior bag but in the process of trying to earn it, you would come across an Hermes Birkin, courtesy social media algorithms, and now you wouldnt know if to keep going and get a Birkin or to just get a Dior and start all over again for a Birkin. Because if you are fond of bags, you would want them both and more - Fendi, Chanel, Louis Vuitton, etc. And then for your Steve Madden heels, you would always have YSLs and Jimmy Choo's. There is no measure to what you would want out of life, only if you let yourself want it. If not shopping then it could be travelling. Himachal would want you to aspire for Banff and Alps. You might ditch Goa for Andamans, but then you would want Maldives, Seychelles and Bora Bora. There is no end to our hearts' desires. But while working towards achieving them, we need to be grateful for what we have. If we keep sulking about what we don't have, the universe knows that we would be sulking no matter what our blessings are. Putting out this kind of negative energy into the cosmos could be harmful. If we are grateful for what we have, we will have a lot more to be grateful for; if we are sulking for what we don't have, then we would have a lot more to sulk about.

Maohi's father had exposed her to all the activities around sports and moving to Hyderabad made her explore other activities like painting, yoga, dancing, etc. In these 2 months, Maohi learnt the value of these activities. One right putt or one finished painting gave her so much joy. All the romantic baggage that she had been carrying started to feel unnecessary and irrelevant. She wasn't done enjoying having enough time on her hands to spend it as she pleased but it was time for her to start her MBA.

3 months into her MBA and Maohi experienced her first "Black Swan" event. In her first lecture of her MBA, she was introduced to the concept of a black swan event. People, for the

longest time in history, didn't know that black swans existed. Only white swans were known until a black swan was spotted in Australia. So, the events that are rare and can't be predicted are called black swan events. The entire country and eventually almost the entire world went under a lockdown when COVID-19 hit.

Chapter - 13

Maohi moved back to Chandigarh during the lockdown. That was the phase when apps like Houseparty, Ludo King, and cult fitness were booming. She and her batchmates would fix days when they would all sync up to get a few drinks on the video call to play these games. On other days, she would go out for her walks, the pollution had dropped, and the air never felt this fresh. There was no traffic on the roads and no heat from the emissions of the vehicles. She started logging 10k-12k steps every day. In her first month of the lockdown, Maohi realised that she loved her own company, provided she was in a safe environment. She also appreciated an occasional glass of red and her mother's homemade lasagna with her parents.

COVID-19 was a turning event in everyone's life. While some dealt with loneliness, others could finally invest in their families or passions or both. Medical professionals were finding it hard to sustain a normal life. Doctors were living out of their

The girl in a pink bow

cars in order to protect their families. Software Engineers who lived within the same countries as their families had flown back home and were working out of the convenience of their homes while others were stuck in isolation. Some were struggling with their mental health due to limited human contact as offices and public spaces were shut. While there were those who were getting to spend more time with their loved ones. There were also those who were bidding farewell to their families in the ICUs. Just like the hospitals, even the crematoriums were overworked. While some small-time PPE kit vendors became rich overnight, there were small-time eateries that went bankrupt. The Epidemic was an example of what fate looked like.

Maohi's neighbour was a 50-year-old man whose 25-year-old son had come home with his 2-month-old baby. The Doctor and his wife had been living alone for about 10 years now. Their son would visit them from time to time but first his education and then his work kept him occupied. Mr. Sethi would live in the outhouse post his hospital hours as he didn't want to risk exposing his family to the virus. All day, he would see patients and their families suffering in the ICUs and cursing COVID but when he got back home, he saw his wife playing with her grandchild. One day, when Maohi was out for her walk, he saw Mr. Sethi driving home from the hospital. He was in the car and he stopped to exchange a few pleasantries with Maohi. Maohi was curious about the situation in the hospital. Mr. Sethi told Maohi that though Chandigarh was doing fairly ok but the patients coming in from different parts of Punjab for their treatment was making it difficult. He gave out some data and figures and how it was only getting worse and there was no sign of things turning around. His daughter-in-law opened the gate. Just when he was about to drive away. He told Maohi, "This time that you are getting with your parents is precious".

Maohi was halfway into her walking routine, she aimlessly wandered for the remaining half about what Mr. Sethi had said. Maohi realised that maybe he was dealing with the most dreadful part of his professional career so far, yet Mr. Sethi was happy to see his grand daughter grow in their front lawn and crawl in their backyard. He was right in the junction of the best and the worst that COVID had to offer. Mr. Sethi was hopping, skipping and jumping between heaven and hell, Daily!

Maohi wondered about her time at home and how this was probably the first time in 5 years that she had spent over 3 months in her house. Her MBA life was in a conundrum. There was no sign of COVID going away, so if she flew out at the first chance she got, she might just be completing her MBA inside the 4 walls of her student apartment. If she deferred, she wouldn't know when she would be able to get out. The uncertainty around COVID-19 brought out the fragility of the systems that we proudly follow. There was no definite way in which this virus was going to proceed; hence, there was no point in pondering. She calmed her anxiety and decided to think about it when she had her visa stamped and the airports were operational. Maohi boarded her flight to Toronto in December 2020, after 7 months of staying at home.

Airports during COVID-19 were in the worst condition ever. Luckily, she at least had a reasonably comfortable experience on her flight from Delhi to Toronto. She wasn't

The girl in a pink bow

expecting the lovely service that she received onboard after her experience at the Delhi airport. Maohi's BSchool had arranged for a shuttle that collected her from the airport and dropped her off at her hotel. All the students had to quarantine for 14 days before they took up their apartments. Maohi reached her hotel in the morning. She was paranoid about spending 14 days locked up in a room. She got an upgrade and she was given a suite with a hot tub in the room. The tub was right next to the glass wall. She could see the entire skyline from her suite on the 14th floor.

Chapter - 14

Maohi settled into her suite. Although she had a fancy hot tub in her room, she just wanted to clean herself nicely after all the travelling and order some room service. She took a long hot water shower and turned on the Television. She was happy that it had Netflix. Maohi started watching "Schitts Creek". She ordered a bowl of aglio olio with some extra bacon and garlic bread on the side. Her meal arrived while she was still on Schitts Creek's 1st episode. Most hotels in the colder regions have hotel rooms that have windows which can't be opened to let in some fresh air. Generally, it's for the sake of optimising the central air conditioning/heating. Places like Toronto don't want to lose the heat generated to the freezing climate outside. Heat loss from the buildings must be a genuine concern for Canada's mission to become carbon neutral.

The idea of not getting any fresh air for 14 days straight is daunting. That was the only thought that bothered Maohi on her first day. She had decided to stay awake, irrespective of sleep deprivation. Maohi didn't want to lose even a day to jetlag. She loved her sunny days and the evenings made her feel slightly gloomy, being locked up by herself in a hotel room would make it worse. She had bought herself some chocolates from duty free, she knew she would be needing some mood elevators when the sun got real low. She stayed awake throughout her first day in Toronto and made sure she lost no time sleeping when the sun was out, the only way to do that was to sync her circadian rhythm to Toronto time.

The hotel's meal delivery system for travelers quarantining was a replica of the meal delivery system of prison. Someone from the housekeeping would knock on her door and would keep a thermocol box with food in it outside her door and Maohi would go and collect it.

Extremely unusual to her normal routine, Maohi got her dinner delivered at 7 PM. She ate her coleslaw sandwich while watching Shitts Creek. Maohi kept her curtains open throughout. The city lights were beautiful. She ate her chocolate while staring out the window and then went to sleep. She had slept for a good 8 hours and woke up to a snowstorm. Maohi had witnessed snowfall only once before, in her childhood when she was holidaying with her parents in London almost 20 years ago, that's when she saw cobble paths covered with snow within an hour.

Maohi walked towards the window and stared at the tiny snowflakes stuck to it, they were the perfect shape and size as if from a Disney movie. She imagined herself to be a princess trapped in a castle and a tiny virus, in her imagination, was now a huge pink dragon guarding her castle door. She opened another bar of chocolate and video-called her mother back home. The only good thing about the time difference was that she could call home in the middle of the night without having to worry about waking her parents. She was still a couple of hours away from her first sunrise in Quarantine. She went back to sleep, dreaming and partly hoping she would wake up in India when she woke up again.

Maohi was woken up by the sunrays, which had become even stronger. The reflection of the sun rays from the snow makes the days even brighter. For Maohi, a bright day was always a happy welcome. After finishing her morning Yoga, Maohi played her instructional video that had all the details on how to monitor your health during COVID and submit your daily temperature on the portal. She heard the knock on the door and she started to walk towards the door with her eyes and concentration on the video playing on her laptop. She opened the door and stepped out to collect her meal. The moment she stepped out of her door and turned to collect her meal, she was startled by an Italian in the opposite room. After 30 hours of isolation, it didn't occur to her that there would be other people in her hotel. Maohi ended up locking herself out. She was wearing a cotton pyjama and a fitted transparent white Ganji. She caught the stranger in the opposite room staring at her. She crossed her hands in front of her chest to cover her breasts, he laughed and apologised half heartedly "sorry but you can't blame me, can you?". Maohi ignored the comment and requested him to call the front desk.

It had been 30 hours since she had checked in and this was the first time she had interacted with a human. She had started

The girl in a pink bow

to feel as if she was living by herself in one of the rooms of an abandoned mansion. Where the ghosts served her meals. Her door was right next to the hallway that led to the elevators, so even if she collected her meals within 2 minutes of the knocking, she never saw anyone.

She stayed in all day, avoiding her charming neighbour and ensuring that she avoided any interaction and delayed collecting her meals. She looked through the peephole before collecting her lunch and dinner to ensure he wasn't around and even after confirming his absence she only stuck out her hand to collect the box.

She woke up the next day and opened her door after 20 minutes of the knock. She was again greeted by the Italian handsomeness. Maohi was collecting her breakfast while he was placing his thermocol box back for housekeeping to collect. As usual, she wasn't appropriately dressed today either. She was in a long black cotton t-shirt and her favourite Garfield undies. The t-shirt was long enough to cover her panties. She tried to bend as gracefully as she could to avoid giving him a peek. Though in her head, she was doing it all too gracefully, the Italian smiled, looking at her awkwardness and chose to give her some space. As soon as he closed his door, Maohi swiftly collected her thermocol box and immediately closed her door.

Though embarrassed by her last 2 interactions, Maohi knew that she wanted to get to know him better and he was her only option for some normalcy during her quarantine. Now Maohi had a mission, She kept looking out the peephole around lunch time. She wanted to open her door in sync with her new crush. She dressed herself in her cutest co ord set. It was a hot pink cord set with hot dogs and burgers printed all over. Maohi decided on her cute yet "not trying too hard" loungewear just before it was time for the next meal. Only once she put it on did she realise that she had hairy legs. Maohi folded her shorts and started to use the razor. She razed her legs while peeping out the peephole. Her legs ended up getting all scratched up. She had more scratches than all the scratches her cat had given her. She was now applying dettol on her wounds while standing and waiting for the Italian to come collect his meal. She finally saw someone in a hotel uniform delivering the meals. The image of Casper knocking and swiftly delivering meals was immediately erased. Italian opened the door after 2 minutes and Maohi ducked immediately, she thought he could see her. Maohi felt silly about ducking and opened her door. He smiled and introduced himself. "Hi, my name is Leonardo and you are?" Maohi introduced herself too. He asked her if she would like to join him for a meal. He said this was his 11th meal that he would be eating by himself, locked up. He had landed from Rome the day before Maohi landed from India. She happily agreed to join him. They didn't want to break any rules because there were high penalties for quarantine breakers. They kept their doors open and put a towel on the floor. He brought a bottle of wine. They both drank an Italian wine out of a disposable glass and ate spaghetti out of a thermocol takeout. Their respective rooms were filled with sunlight and there was a light fragrance of Winter Jasmine from a fresh bouquet of flowers kept on the table that was at the junction of the hallway leading to the elevators and the rooms. Leonardo was an art student and was studying art back home. His father owned a gallery in Rome. He had come for a digital marketing course in

Toronto after completing his undergraduate in arts. His father wanted him to take over the gallery but before doing so, he wanted Leonardo to learn about digital marketing because their gallery's online footprint wasn't that great. Most tourists that visited Rome didn't know of it, which was bad for business. He showed Maohi the pictures of his art gallery and the road that led to it. It was a small cobblestone path that led to a gate covered in grapevines. There was a small vineyard behind the gallery, that's where Leonardo's grandfather did the bottling of the wines and left them for ageing. After his grandfather, Leonardo had taken a keen interest in fashioning recipes for wine. He had been personally bottling and stocking wines for 3 years now, it was a family hobby. The vineyard had a small bar. The few tourists that visited the gallery always stopped at the bar. They purchased their bottles of wine and sometimes drank them at the bar. There was always a spread of charcuterie boards on the centre table. Leonardo enjoyed overhearing the fancy escapades of all the tourists while they sat talking and drinking at his bar.

His phone rang, so he had to cut his conversation short. They retired to their respective rooms. Maohi laid down on her bed and played Schitts Creek. After 30 minutes she woke up to Alex shouting at David. She had slept off and woke up feeling refreshed. She played it again from the previous episode and binge watched it for 3 hours. It was almost dusk but she didn't feel any need to open another bar of chocolate.

She heard the knock on her door again. She opened the door to find Leonardo waiting for her, standing cross-legged and leaning against the frame of the door. He was staring at his

The girl in a pink bow

phone screen when she opened the door. She sat down and they started to eat their meal together. After the meal, he ordered some dessert from a food delivery app. They exchanged a little about their respective countries and cultures. They spoke about EAT PRAY LOVE, where Julia Roberts visits both India and Italy before she finds love in Bali. Was it India and Italy sitting next to each other, loveless? Mention of love brings a touch of sadness to lonely eyes. Maohi wasn't sure if that was what she saw in his eyes or if it was her own projection. Before she could probe any further, Leonardo got a call from his food delivery agent. Housekeeping got them their desserts. Maohi opened her box to find a piece of chocolate cake with dripping nutella and vanilla ice cream. She took a bite of her dessert and savoured the gooey mush in her mouth. They both enjoyed their dessert in silence and then went to bed.

Maohi called her mother to check up on her. Her Father was travelling on business so her mother was by herself at home. Physical distance from a loved one is always painful. Maohi was the only child, and all 3 people in her family were currently in different time zones. Maohi went back to watching Moira Rose complaining about their motel.

We have a lot to thank for the situational comedies. We all keep hearing and reading about what people going through tough times have to say about watching or rewatching F.R.I.E.N.D.S.: heartbreaks, illness, losing a loved one - no matter what it is. The majority of us go back to these shows to catch a break and feel lighter. Two and a Half Men, The Big Bang Theory, How I Met Your Mother, etc. We use their phrases like "Have you met, '___'", "that's what she said", etc. These shows connect people all over the world, and we tend to get a sense of belonging. Globalization has brought the world closer, but being an active participant in the phenomenon can be alienating sometimes. Multiple people from completely different cultural backgrounds and landscapes are brought together into a completely different environment. These immigrants need to gravitate towards each other via happier things than the shared longing of their homes or paranoia of a new world. It's mostly entertainment and sports that bring people together, and that's probably one of their strongest attributes. Watching a bond movie at a theatre, watching Manchester United play Barcelona, ordering in and bingeing F.R.I.E.N.D.S., etc., are the kind of activities that would rarely fail at bringing millennials together.

Chapter- 15

On her 4th day of Quarantine, after a sweaty power yoga session, Maohi decided to fill the hot tub. She Added Blush Berry Cherry and pink grapefruit bath bombs. She also added an extra bubble bath solution. As soon as Maohi fished out her bubble bath solution from her toiletries, she was taken back to her family holiday in Paris. Whenever Maohi travelled internationally with her parents. Her mother always bought her the fanciest bubble baths. The bubble bath bottle would be of vibrant colours with a blingy cap. Her mom would prepare her a bath with her barbies and a million bubbles for Maohi to step in after her tiny feet had walked around alien streets.

They had missed their connecting flight from Paris to Delhi, so Air France Airlines booked them a room in Hilton. Maohi checked in with her mother in the morning and booked the bus tour that took them around Paris and halted near the Eiffel Tower. After they got back from the city tour, to ease their tired bodies from the previous flight and all the walking

The girl in a pink bow

around on the streets of Paris, her mother prepared them a bath with the bubble bath solution that they had bought in Rio. The room at Hilton in Paris had a glass wall similar to the one where Maohi was quarantining and the bubble bath in her hand had the same sparkling silvery glitter cap. Hilton had the view of the runway, so they would see the planes landing and taking off. Maohi's current view was that of Toronto's skyline.

Due to the vibrant colours released by the bath bombs in the tub, the colour of the froth ranged from light baby pink to vibrant plum red. Maohi added lavender-scented bath salts to the bubbly tub. She started the Jacuzzi to mix the solution in the water and millions of bubbles fluttered in her bedroom. She put her hair in a bun and used her bunny ears band to mind her hair before getting into the tub. It felt like stepping into a cotton candy cloud. She sat down, stretched her legs and dropped her head back to relax. The pressure from the nozzles started to massage her entire body. She positioned herself in the tub in a way to derive maximum pleasure. Her body released all of its tension within 10 minutes. She had ordered herself a jar of very berry strawberry ice cream pudding to eat in the tub. After 5 minutes of a shut eye, she unpaused Schitts creek and started to dig into her dessert. The occasional tingle of the bath salts and the oils from the bath bombs added some fun and colour to Maohi's quarantine life. She sat in the tub till her fingers pruned. Then she stepped in for a shower with her vibrator. Maohi cleaned up and got into her bed for a nap.

When she woke up, it was post-lunchtime, and the sky was changing colours just before the Twilight. She laid in bed all cleaned up and relaxed, staring at the sky from her bedroom.

The girl in a pink bow

Maohi stared at the sky during sunset and watched the colours change in the sky till it was dark and the city lights adorned the skyline. She would always spot a different shade of pink or purple or orange or red or blue in the sky during sunsets. Today, she spotted something between purple and blue. She finished her half-eaten bar of chocolate. Her glass wall that overlooked the skyline was still misty from the hot water in her tub. Looking through it felt like staring at an incomplete painting. The parts that were blurred felt like the parts that still needed definition, and the areas where the condensation had cleared were the parts of the painting that were completed. The sunset was not even half there, but the sky was close to completion. She wiped the condensation and completed the painting. Maohi realised she hadn't heard the staff knock at the door to deliver her breakfast, lunch or dinner. She opened the door to check for her meal, but there was nothing at the door either. She went inside and called the reception to find out about her food. The receptionist told her that she would check with housekeeping and get back to her.

Her room's telephone rang, she answered, hoping they would be able to provide something warm to eat because she was starving. It wasn't housekeeping, it was Leonardo. He asked her why she didn't come out for breakfast or lunch and she replied by saying that she never heard the knock and she checked right now but there was no thermocol box either. Leonardo got his box delivered but didn't see Maohi's box at the door. He thought she had collected her food and wanted to eat by herself today. They both decided to get a drink until the hotel figured

The girl in a pink bow

out what had happened to her food. Maohi offered to get her Jack Daniel's, she wanted to have some whisky.

Leonardo hugged Maohi and held her for some time. After he pulled back, his eyes reflected more light than usual. Staying indoors and almost disconnected from the world, Maohi hadn't realised that it was Christmas Eve. Leonardo had been on a video call with his family back in Italy while they prepared their dinner for the eve. He had gotten a little homesick and was hoping to distract himself by speaking to his corridor friend. He was disappointed when he didn't see the meal box. He had to eat his meal by himself, so he got on a video call again while his parents hosted his extended family for a lavish dinner at their bar in the vineyard. He was missing home but could not express it. He was choking while speaking to his parents but the background noise of dinner kept absorbing it. Leo told Maohi that he was hoping for them to hear the choking in his voice so someone would push him to speak up about how he was feeling. He just needed a good cry, a release but it was lost in all the commotion back home. He knew his mother could tell that something was off but she had her hands full. Mother and son were looking at each other, helpless, right before the call was disconnected. She dropped him a text after the call, telling him that she would call him as soon as she could.

Leonardo broke down while talking to Maohi about it, and she consoled him. Maohi's phone rang, and she had to break their embrace. They said there was some confusion. They thought that her lunch was delivered early when someone from the staff had come to deliver her ice cream. Since it was Christmas Eve and there was a lockdown in the city, they

The girl in a pink bow

weren't expecting any guests and their staff had left for the day. The kitchen was anyway understaffed but since it was christmas eve, there wasn't anyone to serve a hot meal. There were a few extra dinner meal boxes, and they delivered the same. Maohi ate her cold burger because she was hungry now. Leonardo was all cried out, and Maohi had eaten her meal. The gloominess that was lingering had started to lift, and they both were feeling at ease. Maohi invited Leonardo in. She said it's Christmas Eve, and the staff can't be that cruel that it would complain about neighbours wanting to spend Christmas Eve together. They watched " The Grinch" and drank their whisky.

Maohi opened her eyes to realise that she was nestled into Leonardo's body and Leonardo had been staring up at her. She looked up at 2 dreamy eyes, staring at her with a goofy smile. Her last memory of the previous night was watching the Grinch steal the Christmas lights and decorations. She was resting her head on Leonardo's shoulder and she apparently passed out and eventually nestled even closer into his body.

It was just after dawn; the sun was out and all of Maohi's vibrant toiletries from her bathtub adventure yesterday were reflecting the sharp sun rays. Leonardo kissed Maohi on her forehead and thanked her for last night. He said, "I was feeling very, very lonely last night. I am so very grateful for you."

Separation Anxiety kicks in almost every time we leave our home to relocate. Festivals, which our entire family has been celebrating together since our childhood, would easily make it to the top 5 of the triggers that can surface separation anxiety. The initial few days just after landing in a foreign land are generally filled with curiosity and excitement. When exciting everyday activities, like eating warm French toast with maple syrup for breakfast while staring out the window when it's snowing, turn mundane. You tend to miss familiarity. For all those who have had the opportunity to relocate and build new lives at multiple places but eventually moved back into their own towns would know that the warmth of the familiarity of our hometown is of the highest quality. We might miss all the places that had started to feel like home, but there is something about the town/city where we grew up.

Leonardo's room had a tiny pantry and he told Maohi that he would go back to his room and order some groceries. "Let me thank you by preparing a Christmas meal for you". He invited Maohi for Christmas lunch to his hotel room. Both of them picked up their respective meal boxes that were delivered for breakfast and took them inside their rooms. Their hotel made their Christmas breakfast Christmassy. Pancakes had reindeer frosting and there was a Christmas tree cookie. Maohi continued Schitts Creek from where she had left it last and enjoyed her little festive meal. While eating her meal, she was mentally going through her clothes that she had packed. She didn't anticipate such an encounter. Hence, she hadn't packed anything fancy in her quarantine bag, she didn't have one matching set of Victoria's Secret in her quarantine bag. She would have to go through her entire luggage to find a cute Christmas outfit. She also would have to come up with a creative Christmas gift. She ordered cupcakes with the frosting that looked like Christmas ornaments and tied a reindeer ribbon to a duty-free bottle of wine. The gift was ready, but Maohi was yet to go through her clothes.

Chapter-16

After an hour of commotion, Maohi sat down to eat her chocolate bar. Her luggage looked like a dumpster ransacked by a raccoon. She still hadn't made up her mind on what to wear. Either the outfit was too over the top or not Christmassy enough or trying too hard or not trying at all or not fitting the vibe (When a European boy is hosting an Asian girl, is there an outfit that would complement a quarantine Christmas lunch date vibe?). She stepped into her shower to clean herself and calm her nerves. She showered and moisturised her body. There was a black dress that was knee length with a slit in front of one thigh. The slit ended right below the seam of her undies. It was a tight-fitting cotton tube dress which flaunted her curves perfectly. If it was only a Christmas lunch and not a date, the dress would mean that Maohi thought of it to be more than just a lunch with a friend. To avoid any awkwardness, she decided to wear a pretty white chiffon dress. It was backless with a halter neck that tied into a cute bow behind her neck. The fabric floated like a feather just below her hips. It was a short flowy dress that she paired with Steve Maiden golden stilettos with a bow in the front. She wore a bright shade of red lipstick and pinched her cheeks for a little colour and plump.

Nothing had happened last night, even though they had slept in the same bed. Maohi didn't know what to make of it. Was Leonardo not attracted to her in that way or was he raised right in a way that he wanted to first take her on a date? She dried her hair and let it fall in natural soft curls and applied her favourite Miss Dior. She collected the cupcakes and a bottle of wine and went over to knock on his door.

Leonardo was dressed in a crisp white shirt and powder pink and light grey chequered pants. He had green eyes and light hazel hair, he must have been around 6 feet 2 inches tall. His hair was short and messy and his beard complimented his jawline. Maohi had never noticed him so intricately, though they had been sharing meals for almost a week now.

She had been admiring him for a while, so to avoid any embarrassment, she dropped her head to the floor before meeting his gaze. "Fuck" Maohi shrieked and slightly jolted her head in disbelief. She saw the bulge in his tailored pants. Until today, he only wore pyjamas, there is no tell until they wear fitted tailor-made pants, not denims but linen/cotton pants. She immediately shifted her gaze further down. He was wearing a pair of gorgeous brown Louis Vuitton shoes that made her Steve Maddens' look casual. Leo was in his date-appropriate outfit and she immediately regretted not wearing her sexy black dress.

The girl in a pink bow

Leonardo asked her what was wrong and she pretended to have forgotten something in the room. He raised an eyebrow and pointed at the door right behind her, all confused, "Something kept 5 steps away CAN NOT be categorised as - 'forgotten'" he definitely disapproved of the dramatic expression. She just handed him the cupcakes and opened the bottle of wine to pour into 2 disposable glasses. Now she was sure that it was a date but she wasn't dressed appropriately for it. She wished she could tell him that the thing that she had forgotten behind was an entire outfit. It might be a relevant excuse for *Simcity* or Virtual Reality dates in the future. Unfortunately, at this point, she would have to just drink some wine and wear an extra awesome personality to compensate for being underdressed. Maohi started flirting with Leo; that was her way of reassuring him that she knew they were on their first date. She either was a terrible flirt or Leo was giving her mixed signals because his reaction to her flirting was mostly confusion or humour. She handed him his glass of wine and they both clinked, as much as a disposable can clink, "Merry Christmas". His room had a 2-chair table set, instead of a jacuzzi, next to a glass wall. The skyline was completely different, his view had the CN Tower. Leo had put out a vanilla-scented candle but they both agreed against lighting it to avoid fire alarms.

His phone rang and now that enough people have iPhones, we all can identify a facetime. He answered the video call and a girl greeted him, "Hello, love!". Maohi had watched enough Hollywood to hope that the girl who just called Leonardo "love" was anyone but a romantic interest. That thought vanished before it could even formulate ****POOF****. Leonardo responded, "Hello baby, Maohi just walked in for the Christmas lunch". The pink from Maohi's cheeks vanished as she started to grow pale, she could feel her face discolouring so she immediately gulped all the wine hoping the heat would compensate for, now almost evaporating, romantic blush. Leonardo, without much of a warning, rotated the camera and introduced Giulia. She had placed her phone on her kitchen island, with the camera facing her while she seasoned her baked pasta.

Giulia was a beautifully dull woman. She had lovely, long, straight, jet black hair that gave a perfect frame to her oval face. Her chin and cheekbones could cut solitaire into two perfect diamonds. She was white like milk with little to no colour, which made her big black eyes pop. She looked like a beautiful vampire being preserved over centuries. A slightly crooked nose which didn't gather any attention because her perfect lips hogged all of it. Giulia's smile didn't touch her eyes and Maohi wondered if that was out of a tinge of underlying envy or if it was just her cold personality. They shared formal pleasantries. Then Leonardo jumped in to tell Maohi that Guilia would be joining them for lunch.

Guilia carried her pasta to her living room. Maohi could see white curtains and white couches with white feather cushions. She opened the curtains and the moment sunlight touched her face, Maohi thought she sparkled and waited for her to burn up in flames. Unfortunately, none of it really happened. Leonardo brought their Christmas lunch, it looked exactly like the pasta that Guilia had baked. Leonardo assured Guilia that a chair was set aside for her but for operational feasibility, he would place his iPhone against a napkin holder on the table. Maohi could see herself and Leonardo, with a backdrop of a CN tower skyline, on the phone screen. Until now, she had never noticed how clean the hotel windows were. They all poured themselves another round of wine and toasted to health and happiness.

Maohi realised that Leonardo had been updating Guilia about all their meetings. The conversations between Maohi and Leonardo were a continuation of their conversation from the last couple of days and Guilia could not only follow but also be an active participant. The only part that was missed out was about the last night that Leo had spent with Maohi. The moment Guilia complained about Leonardo not calling her last night, he said something in Italian. She responded in Italian and Maohi didn't understand a word. She could sense some revulsion trying to sneak out, like a tiny green beast, through Guilia's tone and expression while she tried to maintain her poise. She knew that Leo was in Maohi's room but the part where she woke up nestled into his arms was carefully camouflaged.

We tend to tell white lies in order to avoid uncomfortable situations. How white are these lies, after all? Isn't there always a tiny hint of grey in them? The more we get comfortable with these discretions, the darker the grey becomes. But unfortunately that's the only way out through such complications.

Relationships between opposite genders can occasionally be more wholesome than a relationship between the same genders. This probably could be because there is absence of competition. We have a conscience that, if used properly, can help us all celebrate our opposite sex relationships without any insecurity or jealousy from our partner. Just a conscious effort not to give into a fleeting moment of weakness or sexual attraction. Prioritising our partner's feelings over our natural instincts could help us have an honest and healthy relationship with our partner. While maintaining all our lovely affiliations with the opposite sex without any awkwardness. But there are times when we might be on a slippery slope. If the relationship isn't fulfilling, then the inclinations toward strangers start to lurk in the dark gray.

Chapter - 17

Guilia had to hang up because it was time for her to prepare her Christmas Lunch in Italy. Maohi and Leonardo sat in silence for a bit as each pretended to eat their cupcake. Maohi wanted to get rid of the silence and wanted to finally get on to her Christmas Lunch with her *FRIEND*. Though they had nothing to hide but Guilia's video call had created an unexplainable discomfort. Maohi could see imaginary black clouds all over the place with Guilia's name written in sparkles on them. She started to wave her hands frantically to disperse them. Leonardo looked up at her and she pretended to be dispersing some unpleasant odour. "Do you think something is burning in the pantry?" Leonardo raised an eyebrow and smirked and then started to laugh because Maohi had the funniest expression on her face. Trying to overcompensate for when we are caught in our silliness, we start over-acting and it ends up being comical. Leonardo just nodded in disapproval while he laughed. "I don't smell anything but that could just be a symptom of COVID-19; that's what we are quarantining for, after all. Let me check the pantry anyway". As he walked away, Maohi started to actively get rid of unsettling imaginary Guilia clouds by frantically moving her hands to hush them away from different parts of the room. Leo came back from the pantry with a calmer expression. The unease from the room had finally disappeared. They opened another bottle of wine and everything went back to how it was. This was Leonardo's last bottle.

Over the next 1 week, they continued to have their meals sitting opposite to each other from their respective doors.

One evening, when Maohi was on her health update call, the fire alarm went off. Either someone was smoking in the room or the hotel thought that people needed some fresh air and what better day than New Year's Eve to let them all out. Maohi and Leonardo went down the staircase and stepped out of the building. It was snowing. They decided to go for a small walk before going back to their rooms. Leonardo got 2 cigarettes on his way down; they both shared the first and then the second cigarette in the next 30 minutes. Though the hotel staff had instructed everybody to get back to their rooms after 20 minutes, they lingered a little longer. The elevators had long queues. Once the front lobby had cleared up, they decided to climb up the stairs anyway and took another 10 minutes talking and chilling and resting in between.

Leonardo told her that this was his last night in the quarantine, he had checked in on the 19th and Maohi had checked in on the 20th. He had asked a friend of his to pick him up 1st late night. As soon as the clock changed the date, and it was the 2nd in their systems, he could check out. Before

Leonardo had even landed in Toronto, he had asked a friend of his to pick him up on the 1st. He wanted to get out of quarantine as soon as he could. "I couldn't have even imagined in the wildest of my dreams that I would have preferred staying back another night," Leonardo confessed. Maohi wanted to ask him to stay another night. She didn't.

Maohi and Leonardo followed each other on Instagram that night. She stalked his profile to find if he had any photos with Guilia; he didn't. Guilia's profile was private, so she couldn't tell if she had posted him. Though Maohi had been on Instagram for over 2 years now, she had started to actively use it only during COVID. Before that, she had posted no more than 2 posts and she had learned during COVID about the multiple features of posting stories like background songs, filters, stickers, etc. She wasted enough time scrolling through Instagram and Facebook but she rarely posted or shared.

Though Leo was busy all day packing, he didn't miss his meals with Maohi. He knocked at her door before leaving to hug her and thank her. Leonardo said, "I could never imagine anything good coming out of this Pandemic, and then I met you in my Quarantine." He hugged her tightly, he planted a soft kiss on her cheeks. They looked at each other for a few seconds while they were in each other's embrace. It was more of a promise in their eyes, the promise to culminate their intentions if and when the opportunity presented. Today, he had to keep the respect of his relationship.

They said their goodbyes and Maohi closed her door. She leaned against her door, knowing that he would be standing a second longer resting his hand against the door. She looked through the peephole and saw his head drop. She could tell he knew that she was looking, he looked up at the peephole and gave her a reassuring smile and left. His smile thawed the coldness that had started to frost and shackle her heart. The warmth gave her cheeks a cherry tint. She smiled with her heart and eyes and unwrapped her last bar of chocolate. As soon as she took her first bite, her phone chimed.

Instagram

LeoNArtDuo: 1 image

He sent her the image of the front gate. "Get out soon, This world needs you now."

Maohi immediately called her friend to have her picked up at midnight the next day instead of the day after.

Chapter-18

Maohi's friend Andy reached her hotel at 11:50 PM on the 2nd of Jan and she checked out at midnight. By 12:05 AM, she was driving away and clicked the same photo of the exit gate that Leo had sent her on his way out and sent it to him. Maohi was craving good Indian food and she asked Andy to order her some Spicy *masala chicken* with *garlic naan*. Andy was living in a cute 2-bedroom apartment with a beautiful backyard. It was snowing and the temperatures had dropped to -5C but as soon as she stepped out of Andy's car, she stood in his backyard, watching the snowfall and breathing her fresh air of freedom. Andy opened his house and turned the heating on, he opened 2 bottles of beer. After sticking to wine and whisky during her quarantine, Maohi had been craving some good Canadian beer. She had asked Andy to get her some before he came to pick her up. Andy and Maohi were college friends. Andy, Shard and Maohi always hung out together. He was the first one to know about Shard and Maohi getting romantically involved in college. But they hadn't been in touch for a while and had a lot of catching up.

Maohi decided to take a long hot water shower and change into her night clothes. She finished her beer and stepped in for a shower. Quarantine was more like a part of her travel. Her hotel stay felt like a transit, another travel experience. But now that she was bathing in a house in Brampton, it suddenly started to feel too real. The toiletries on the bathroom shelves and the counter were nothing like what she had at home. Now that she was not using the products out of the dispensers of the hotel or her travel kit, she suddenly missed her home. This was probably the first time Maohi felt homesick since she had landed in Canada. She started weeping in the shower. She kept it as low as she could in order to avoid any uneasy conversations.

The part of human psychology that is troubling is how we shy away from crying in front of people. We can share a good laugh with a stranger on the road but some of us struggle with our tears even in the comforts of our closest friends and families. Is it because we want to be by ourselves and not answer questions? Or is it because we want to be able to cry without being asked to "stop crying" in order to not to make anyone around us uncomfortable?

Once Maohi's weeping had turned into sobs, she was ready to dry up and put on a brave face. She wore her night suit and stepped out. The moment she stepped out, she could smell Indian gravies - food, as always, improved her mood. Andy had laid some cutlery with the takeout on the kitchen island. She served herself and opened another bottle of beer. Andy could tell the heaviness in her voice and eyes was from an emotional

The girl in a pink bow

downpour in the shower. He played stand-up comedy on the TV while they ate and spoke about their time in college. Shard had finally made it to Canada and was actively in touch with Andy. They spoke a little about Shard and how his life had changed since they parted ways. Maohi eventually passed out on the couch while watching TV.

She woke up to a strong sun in her eyes. It was a beautiful winter morning. She felt as if the sun was shining to give Maohi a warm welcome into her new life. Andy took Maohi driving around in the streets of Downtown Toronto. It wasn't as bustling as one would see on Instagram reels, Andy had warned to expect this because of COVID. They took some takeout for brunch and ate in the car. Then they started to head for her student housing, her accommodation in the university. Maohi had made some lovely friends in her MBA batch for whatever time they all got in Hyderabad before the university locked down due to COVID-19.

She was excited to reunite with them as these people were going to be her little family in a foreign land. She reached her apartment building right after sunset and entered her building. Her apartment building had the buzzer system just like she saw in most of the 80s and 90s rom-coms she had watched throughout her life. Maohi had fantasised about a lover buzzing her while she got ready to take her out on the first date and one day used the same buzzer system to confess his love to her. After buzzing in, she stood there, dreaming about Leo standing there with sunflowers in his hands and expressing his raw, unfulfilled desires from their night at the hotel. Before she could respond, Maohi heard her flatmate from the apartment intercom: "Hi,

The girl in a pink bow

who is this?". And Maohi was pulled back into reality. She responded, "Maohi" with a faint dullness.

Maohi's apartment was in a 20-story building with duplex penthouses on the 19th and 20th floors. It was a red brick building with an entrance that had a white porte cochere. The residents had an access card that they had to swipe to get in. All the guests had to buzz in by pressing the button next to the respective apartment numbers on the right wall of the vestibule. You could speak with the person you were visiting through the apartment intercom. Only when a resident gave access to a guest could the guest get into the lobby. The lobby had elevators and a staircase.

Suvreen had already moved into their apartment and had set up her room. It had only been 2 days, so there was bare minimum in the living area and the kitchen. Though everything was functional, it felt nothing like home.

Maohi had packed a bedsheet with pineapples on it, her favourite bedsheet that she used at home. She had packed it with her to feel at home when she hit the bed every night. From her past experience of moving away from home, she had come to realise that it hits the hardest when you rest your head on the sheets and the sheets don't feel like home. Just like we hold onto our lover's clothes because their natural scent is woven in the fabric. Maohi took her home with her, woven in the fabric of her linens. She pulled her sheet from her luggage and spread it on her bed. Green pineapples brought the room to life, it was nothing close to home but something warm and happy.

The girl in a pink bow

She unpacked the bag she had opened to pull out the pineapples. She left the other bag as is. It was already midnight. She lost track of time and it slipped her mind that she was invited for dinner at one of her batchmates' penthouse.

Mehul, Jordan, Mikhail and Saurabh were Maohi's home away from home in Toronto. Mehul and Saurabh had taken up the penthouse in the same building and Mikhail and Jordan were in the adjacent apartment. Maohi had told them that she would be coming but she had forgotten to tell them that she reached. It was only around midnight that she realised that they had been calling her while she was busy unpacking. Before she could call back, she heard a knock on the door. Suvreen was out visiting a friend and this was the first time Maohi was receiving someone in her new apartment. It was Mikhail, "Where have you been, you dumbass?" the entire floor could hear him complaining. Maohi jumped with excitement and hugged Mikhail and Jordan. She explained how she wanted to do a bit of bedding to make sure she returned back to something familiar and she had lost track of time while unpacking a few things.

The penthouse on the 19th and 20th floor had 2 balconies. The living area opened into a balcony and the master bedroom on the 20th floor had an attached balcony. Maohi and Suvreen skipped an extra semester due to COVID and their visa issues. But most of them had moved to Toronto 6 months ago including Mehul and Saurabh. Hence, the penthouse was a fully functional household. There were chilled beers in the fridge and grilled chicken in the Oven. All of them ate all their meals together, irrespective of their living arrangement. They

The girl in a pink bow

updated Maohi on what was new and what Toronto was like. They guided her with a few of the necessities that could come in handy. She kept making mental notes to act upon them in the coming week. After some beers and grilled chicken, she went back to her apartment. She was so glad that she had made her bed and unpacked a bit earlier. She dozed off as soon as her head hit the pillow.

Chapter-19

Maohi's room had a huge window and a curtain that did very little to keep the daylight out. She woke up slowly around 9 AM. It had snowed a little early in the morning. She stepped into the living room to find the house empty. Maohi preferred quiet mornings. She went into the kitchen and fixed herself some coffee. She hadn't noticed their balcony the previous night. It was right opposite the kitchen. She opened the curtains and saw the university buildings, partially covered in snow. She fetched herself an overcoat because she wanted to step out onto the balcony for her coffee. She was hoping that the winds wouldn't be too unkind. Fortunately for her, it wasn't a very windy day. Though it was extremely cold and she had to pull up her overcoat's hood, it was comfortable enough to finish a cup of coffee. The view from her window was the same as the view from the balcony. The air was fresh and crisp on this quiet winter morning. Maohi had 1 more week to go before her classes started. She decided to take a hot water shower and explore the campus.

Mehul wanted to get some groceries from the on-campus grocery store, so he offered to show Maohi around. He took her around the university. It was a huge campus. One side of the road was the housing area. There were different housing concepts. He showed her independent villas, which were further divided into family housing and bachelors. The family section gave out the entire villa to one person, whereas the bachelors rented out individual rooms in the villas. Then there were mixed-use buildings, where there were cute cafes or various stores on the ground floor and the apartments were above them. They decided to get coffee from one of the cafes before exploring the lecture halls, sports complex and other campus buildings.

Most of the cafes were shut and only a few were serving takeouts. There were hardly any people around and only 1 person working at the counter. Multiple rules came out during COVID related to lockdown and the eventual reopening. It became complicated to keep track of what would be open and when. One of the directions included the capacity at which the essential and non-essential categories could operate. These capacities also varied based on the Zone in which the outlet was located. Different zones were created based on the spread of the virus in those areas. Different areas kept getting into different zones as the number of infected population kept fluctuating in the area. Few businesses chose to remain temporarily closed if the restrictions, like limiting indoor capacity to 20%, didn't make business sense. They would have to clean the entire area and keep it warm. They couldn't restrict a few people in one area because there were rules around social distancing indoors. It was all too chaotic. Maohi's university was far from the most crowded area, the downtown area. So when the students stepped out in and around their campus, they could at least get some decent coffee. She posted her coffee with the backdrop of her university campus on her Instagram story. Her first story since she got out of her quarantine. Her second since she landed in canada.

Her first story after landing was about the pancakes and maple syrup served to her for her breakfast during her quarantine. She had added a polling feature to that story -

Could this breakfast "BE" any more Canadian?

No

Yes, I have a lot to learn and break my stereotypical judgements.

Mehul and Maohi loitered around for a bit, he showed her the different departments in the university and the sports complex. The sports complex was shut and of course, the buildings were empty. Even the Admin block had been working from home for almost a year now. They felt sad about not being able to attend the lectures in person. An MBA degree has a lot to do with peer-to-peer learning. We have to be present in the classrooms to make the most of our MBA lectures. It isn't something we can do on a system sitting alone in our rooms. But unfortunately, that's what it was going to be like for this batch. They had seen videos and photos of the campus that they were crossing and they could only imagine what the campus

The girl in a pink bow

would have looked like with all the students and staff walking around. For now, it was just the 2 of them crossing deserted halls and corridors.

Mehul had decided to pick up the groceries after completing Maohi's tour of the campus; he didn't want to carry the bags around. After exploring the campus area for 2 hours, they decided to head back and go to the grocery store. The grocery stores were allowed to operate at a maximum capacity of 50% occupancy. The customer had to follow social distancing from all the other customers in the grocery store who didn't belong to the same household. There were small circles marked to line up for billing, these circles kept people from breaking social distancing while queuing up to pay. Each person (or a household unit) had to occupy the spot behind the customer in front of them. There were lines outside grocery stores to enter and these lines also had similar circles. Customers had to wait outdoors if the store was at maximum capacity. Only when someone stepped out could they step in. Most of the cafes and bakeries were only allowing takeouts. Due to this reason, students seldom went to grocery stores and mostly got it delivered at home. There were online apps that you could place an order on and the grocery would get delivered the next day. But if you wanted something within a couple of hours, there was no other option but to go to the store. Mehul enjoyed cooking, so if he had his mind on something that he wanted to cook, he would step out to get the missing ingredients. But waiting outside the stores during winters in bone chilling winds was always painful.

By the time it was spring, all these restrictions had started to ease.

Students had to choose their subjects, and once they chose all the subjects for that semester, they could generate a timetable. Based on this timetable, all 5 of them had decided to take up 2 meals per week to cook for the rest. There were five of them and 10 meals to be cooked, Monday to Friday. Lunch and dinner were cooked at home and on weekends most of them socialised with other batch mates or had date nights. Mehul found his Monday and Thursday afternoons free, so he opted to cook lunch on Monday and Thursday. His and Maohi's coffee runs and grocery shopping became a Monday and a Thursday ritual. They could see cafes and restaurants slowly coming back to life. Towards the end of the spring, these places were getting prepared to host.

One Thursday morning, the patios had started to reopen. Maohi and Mehul saw multiple bakeries serving scrumptious meals. The more patios they crossed, the hungrier they got looking at the food on the tables. Every bakery smelled like a little dessert heaven with a hint of freshly ground coffee beans. They decided to stop at a bakery that had chocolate-filled croissants. Mehul and Maohi entered the bakery and they were transported to the candy house from Hansel and Gretel. They could only see the chocolate-filled croissant shelf from the window and they weren't prepared for what they saw when they entered. One wall had sections of croissants with multiple fillings. There were at least 10 different types of croissants with fillings like blueberry sauce, caramel, hazelnut, Nutella, pistachio, etc. The other wall had shelves of different muffins -

The girl in a pink bow

blueberry, raspberry, chocolate, banana, vanilla, etc. The wall parallel to the glass window and door had croissants, and the wall perpendicular had muffins. The wall opposite the muffins had freshly baked breads - garlic, wheat, cranberry and pumpkin seeds, banana, focaccia, etc. All were stacked next to each other and adjacent to the counter. They also had different chocolates in glass jars that were displayed above the shelves that stored breads. Unlike the witch in the fairytale (Hansel and Gretel), they were greeted by a charming lady who must have been in her 60s. It was a bakery run by an old Italian couple. There was some indoor seating but they chose to be on the patio. There was snow out on the street and the sun frequently peeked from behind the clouds. The weather was pleasant.

They placed their orders. Maohi ordered a sunny side up with a slice of focaccia and Mehul ordered a cheese omelette with a slice of garlic bread. They also ordered a muffin and a croissant with an americano each and requested the old lady to serve the coffee with the muffins before serving the eggs. Mehul ordered a nutella croissant and Maohi ordered a banana muffin. Luckily, the clouds cleared the moment they took their seats, they clicked a few pictures with and of their food. Maohi posted them on her Instagram story. By now, she had obsessively started to check if Leonardo was in the viewers list of her stories. Since the bakery was run by Italians, Maohi had added a cryptic text too - "Everytime an Italian feeds me, a fairy gets an upgrade on her pixie dust". Hoping he would reply to her story. So far, he was at the top of her viewers list.

Though no one but the developers who write the algo for displaying the viewers list on our story know how the list is

The girl in a pink bow

populated. Yet some of us have imagined that the viewer on the top is someone who has interacted the most with our profile. It could also be the viewer whose profile we have interacted with the most. The algo also keeps updating; one could believe that the initial 6-7 viewers are the ones who have recently viewed our story and the rest are stacked based on the level of their interaction, or our interaction or a mean of how much we have interacted with each other. There could be endless assumptions but that's all that they are, assumptions. It's not like we had less reasons to get anxious about our romantic interests in the real world but now the virtual world has our anxiety on steroids. In the real world, we do catch a break, and we're able to disconnect because we are helpless. But Social media is always accessible.

Chapter - 20

Maohi had spent winter and spring building networks, as she had decided to take summer off so she could intern and travel. Since the restrictions hadn't eased completely, the workspaces were mostly Hybrid. She interviewed for a company and negotiated a decent stipend for herself. Her MBA had 4 semesters and 1 internship. Just before she winded up submissions and exams for her 3rd semester, she had sorted her finances and an itinerary to travel.

As soon as her batch turned in their last assignments, the entire building had converted into one big club. The deadline for all the submissions was midnight, so no one had any plans of going out to party and every apartment had their alcohol stocked the previous weekend. 40% of the apartments on every floor had their doors open for people to drop in and chill. Every apartment had a different vibe but joy and relief were common elements. Maohi and Suvreen wanted to unwind before they stepped out to experience the building's vibe. They opened a beer each and sat on their balcony. Just before they could finish their cans, Jordan and Mikhail entered their home with a Bluetooth speaker in the shape of a boombox. 4 of them sat and finished their first drink of the night. They opened their second cans and then they stepped out of the apartment and went in different directions. Maohi cruised through multiple apartments of the building to meet the friends and teammates that she had attended lectures with and had done group assignments with. She and her friends were to gather at Mehul's penthouse after an hour.

Maohi had made friends with people from different corners of the world. Though she had a one-sided ongoing affair with Leonardo's Instagram account, she had developed small crushes in different lectures. While she would be attending her classes online, she would scan through all the people on the webcam. Whenever some testosterone caught her eye, she took a screenshot and sent it to her WhatsApp group. Mehul had created a WhatsApp group to coordinate lunches and dinners, but Maohi used it to broadcast her romantic interests and enquire about them. She had liked a guy from Russia, one from Sri Lanka and a Latino. Out of all 3, Javiar from Mexico was the one she had been actively interacting with throughout the winter semester. Out of the 6 lectures that she had every week, he was in 4 of her classes. He lived in the penthouse adjacent to Mehul's. Maohi and Javiar would study together, complete assignments together and on most days, they even got their coffee before class from the same place. When the temperature started to rise and it started to get warmer, Javiar and Maohi started to step out to get some donuts and a cup of coffee from

The girl in a pink bow

Tim Hortons and then attended their lectures together from a park. They would do it whenever it was sunny outside.

Eventually, the sports complex and the gym reopened. The swimming pool had opened up and they had started to go for a swim every evening. Because of the COVID restrictions, students had to book a slot every time they wanted to go swimming. Javiar and Maohi always booked their slots when they were together to ensure that they got the same slot.

Javiar was a fashion designer who was doing a course in luxury management at the University. Javiar and Maohi were in Human Behaviour, Strategy, Operations and Data Analytics classes together. She helped him with Operations and Data Analytics, and he helped her with Human Behaviour and Strategy.

They had started to build a strong connection, and Maohi looked forward to running into him whenever she went up to the penthouse for her meals. Planned interactions are never as exciting as unplanned ones. She would run into him on his floor unknowingly, and every time that happened, she felt like a teenager in the 90s. When there was no social media and running into your crush was just another prayer answered.

By the time everyone met at the penthouse, it was 2 AM but Maohi was MIA. Mikhail had last seen her with Susie from the 10th floor. Susie was in Mikhail and Maohi's Marketing class. They had just submitted their final group assignment. Mikhail had to go for a game of beer pong. Susie's neighbours were one player short, so they had been bribing Mikhail to help complete the team. That was the last that Mikhail had seen

Maohi and she had told him that she would be going to the penthouse after finishing her beer. But she wasn't there.

The music was loud in the penthouse and everyone was drinking and dancing. Everyone forgot about Maohi and they started to reminisce about their time in Hyderabad. There was a group of students in Hyderabad who got together after the submission of every assignment and drank, irrespective of what day it was. They would submit the assignment at midnight and then gather to get drunk. The same group of people, except Maohi, were chilling in the penthouse for the first time since they had landed in Canada. Back in Hyderabad, there was only one batch and all the students had the same submissions and assignments. But now people had different subjects, timelines, assignments, submissions, etc. the previous semester didn't have all the students in canada because few of them were stuck due to some or the other issue or they just decided to not to risk travelling in COVID or they were hopeful that things would open up and they might be able to attend in-person classes.

But today, the entire batch was finally in and the semester had ended for everyone, irrespective of the subjects, on the same day. People had felt isolated and distant due to COVID-19 and mismatched schedules. They had all been waiting for an evening like this.

After some time, they all decided to head out. It wasn't as cold anymore and it was a lovely full moon night. Just when Mehul was about to lock the apartment, it struck him that Maohi was nowhere to be seen. He reached out to Suvreen to

The girl in a pink bow

ask her if she knew where Maohi was but she pretended to be clueless.

Maohi had texted Suvreen that she was with Javiar but she didn't want anyone to know about it. Javiar had quite a reputation, people thought of him to be a player. He was 5 feet 11 inches tall. He looked like a Latino version of Peter Andre from Mysterious Girl. He had deep brown hair and the dreamiest eyes one could ever look into. Javiar played guitar and sang. If he was asked to play at any gathering, he always looked into the eyes of the girl sitting closest to him when he sang. Most girls had claimed to have fallen for him in those 3-4 minutes. Javiar never did that to Maohi. She always thought that he wasn't romantically inclined towards her and that their relationship was platonic. She would see him flirt with random girls at different parties.

At least 4-5 apartments in the building always had a group of 6-10 people listening to music and chilling on any given day of the week. And Maohi and Javiar would land up in the same apartment at least once every 2 weeks. That's the only time they ever interacted while intoxicated. Maohi would become chatty after a can of beer and Javiar would just listen to her speak. He was full of energy and enthusiasm all the time but very quiet and intense around Maohi whenever they were intoxicated. Maohi thought she probably bored him to death, which was why he was awfully quiet around her at the parties. He would be all chirpy with everyone else but her. On all other days, they would mostly be actively involved in swimming, classes, coffee, etc. They never just sat and talked; their love for coffee and swimming and the overlapping classes were the only reasons

The girl in a pink bow

why they hung out as frequently as they did. But now that the session had ended, she wasn't sure if this would continue any further.

Everyone started to look for Maohi, and Suvreen had to be part of the search party even though she knew that Maohi was safe and fine. Suvreen tried to call Maohi but Maohi's phone was switched off. After searching a few apartments and calling a few people, they started to look for her outside the building. Maohi liked to spend some time by the lake at least once every day. That's where everyone started to head towards, it was a beautiful spot. When they didn't find Maohi at the lake, they decided to abort their mission and sat by the lake.

Suvreen was standing on one end of a rock that everyone was sitting on and she felt a pebble hit her back. She ignored it the first time but then when it happened again, she looked behind and saw Javiar and Maohi standing in the bushes and she could tell that they were naked. Maohi pointed at a tree and Suvreen looked at it and realized that their clothes were under a tree that was beyond the rock. Luckily, everyone had settled on the rock and walked past it. Suvreen pretended to be on a call and stepped aside. She picked up their clothes but dropped Maohi's Bra in haste. She quietly threw all the other clothes in the direction of the bushes while she distracted everyone by urging them to look at the moon. She kept them occupied by telling a random story about that particular full moon. Maohi and Javiar had managed to dress themselves by then and Maohi joined all of them and Javiar went back to his apartment. He didn't want anyone to see them together. Maohi was dying to share with Suvreen about the night she had had with Javiar.

The girl in a pink bow

No matter how close a girl-boy bond is, a girl is always more excited to share about her romantic escapades with her girlfriends. She knows that only another girl can understand and experience what she is trying to explain.

The next morning, Suvreen was drinking her coffee when Maohi walked into the apartment. Suvreen demanded to know all about last night. What happened before she smuggled her clothes for her and after everyone dispersed from the lake? Where had she been and what had been going on. Maohi made herself a cup of coffee and they both sat on the balcony. Maohi was excited to speak about her night in the desire of wanting to live it all over again.

Chapter-21

After Mikhail left Maohi at Susie's, Maohi hung around with Susie, discussing their plans for the summer. Both of them were taking summer off and interning. Maohi had plans to travel, and Susie wanted to know more about Maohi's itinerary and the research that she had done on protocols around travelling during COVID-19. They got all pumped up and excited about their summer plans and toasted its commencement with a few shots of tequila. Maohi left Susie's. She had always been extremely fond of travelling, she always got super excited when discussing her travel plans. By now, her face was beaming.

After leaving Susie's, Maohi decided to go to the Penthouse. The moment she stepped on their floor, she bumped into Javiar. All the students who were bumping into each other that night were apartment-hopping with a can of beer. Javair was going back to his penthouse after a jam session. His apartment was always filled with fancy people. They were

The girl in a pink bow

all from luxury management and tonight would have been no different because penthouses were the largest apartments in the building and most of the students ended up eventually hanging at one of the penthouses because only they could accommodate larger gatherings. Javiar took Maohi's can to take a sip of what she was drinking and the moment he realised that it was empty, he dragged her into his apartment.

She was right, his apartment was full of fancy shmancy elites. He took her to his room so she could pick a drink for herself. The weather had just started to get better and Maohi loved her beers. Unfortunately, his bed was covered in cans of premixed cocktails. She picked a cute pink can with a pineapple on it. He pulled out a can of JD and Coke. They opened their cans and toasted to their first summer in the country. Before she could even swallow, he kissed Maohi. He pulled away and accepted that he hadn't had a tastier drink. He took her back to his party. Maohi wasn't sure about what to do next. She followed him down to the living area. And he made her sit next to him. Never in the last 4 months did he ever even sit next to her at any social event. Today, he made sure that every 10 minutes he held her hand and he pulled her towards him to make sure that their bodies were in constant contact even when they were speaking to other people. If he didn't feel Maohi next to his body even for a second, he looked around with a look of panic in his eyes and pulled her closer to him again. There was barely any light in the apartment and people were too busy to notice what was going on. Maohi, on the other hand, was struggling to hold a conversation with anyone else; her heart was beating in her ears. The pace at which it was beating was

The girl in a pink bow

the only thing that she was able to focus on. Maohi realised that she had been away from her friends for quite some time now and she stood up to go to the penthouse next door.

Before she could even start her sentence, Javiar told her that she was not going anywhere out of his sight tonight. She tried to explain that her friends would be waiting. Maohi didn't want them to know that she was with Javiar. He told her that she wasn't going anywhere. That is when Maohi dropped Suvreen a text to tell her about where she was. Maohi went out to the balcony because the atmosphere was starting to get overwhelming for her. These people were not her friends and she had nothing in common with any of them. Maohi needed her friends and her people but she was loving the importance and attention that she was getting. So she just stepped out onto the balcony. She had hardly stepped out when Javiar called out to her from behind. He stepped out onto the balcony with her and shut the balcony door.

He asked her if something was wrong. He was worried and she could tell. He said "Now is not the time to discuss what happened or to explain myself. I would die of guilt thinking that maybe I did something wrong and that is why you are choosing to leave", he paused but Maohi didnt react so he continued "If you leave now I would assume that kiss was a mistake because had you liked it then you would have chosen to stick around in the hopes of sneaking in another one". Maohi opened her mouth to explain herself, but he told her that anything that she said would feel like an excuse to get rid of him. He begged her to not to leave his side, just for tonight. She agreed but told him that she was feeling out of place and she would rather just

The girl in a pink bow

be with him. He smiled, and Maohi could tell that the muscles in his body that had been tense all this while were finally relaxed.

Javiar told his friends that he had to go drop Maohi at one of the villas and that he would be back in a bit. Not that they seemed to care. They both stepped out and Maohi sprinted through the hallway to avoid running into anyone. They got into the lift and started to kiss, the slight fear of the lift stopping and someone entering made the moment exciting. Luckily the lift took them directly to the ground floor.

Both of them started to walk towards the lake. He told her that he agrees that she might be finding all of this too confusing and he was going through similar emotions as well, but he suggested to think about it tomorrow. She obediently agreed and started to talk about random things that were going on in the building. There were apartments that had bubbles coming out of their doors. Some apartments had disco balls for lights. Javair mentioned a couples-only gathering, there were no singles allowed. He wasn't sure if that was an arrangement with an expectation to swap partners or if it was for the couples that had dealt with infidelity in the past and now being around singles with their partners made them insecure. Before they could finish all their stories from tonight, they had reached the lake. It was a very clean lake, and the water was crystal clear. It had a small area that had sand, and it looked like a tiny beach.

The first thing that Maohi blurted out and immediately regretted was "I have never gone skinny dipping". It was a beautiful night and the moonlight was reflecting on the water in the lake. Javiar started to undress Maohi. Maohi was wearing

The girl in a pink bow

a white cotton sweatshirt and denim shorts. He lifted her sweatshirt to expose her breasts through a lacy red bra. It had been almost 2 years since Maohi had even kissed a man. Now she was standing stark naked in front of the dreamiest boy. He undressed himself he pulled his boxers. They both stepped into the lake slowly to avoid making any sound of splashing. Once they were in, he took Maohi's face in his hands and started to kiss her again. They kissed for forever and it felt like they slipped into a different world.

Suddenly, they heard a few people talking and approaching the lake. Both of them freaked out and got out of the water from the opposite side where there were bushes so they could hide. They were hiding from the guards behind the bushes, only to eventually realise that it was Maohi's friends looking for her. She felt a little guilty about ditching them.

That's when Suvreen came to their rescue, and Maohi joined her friends braless. Javair had given her his shirt to dry her body. Her hair was still soaking wet. She told them that after Susie's, she was on her way to Mehul's penthouse but someone spilled some cheese on her hair in the lift. So she had to go back to her apartment and wash it off. By the time she went back to the penthouse they all had left.

After everyone got back from the lake, Maohi charged her phone and switched it on. She had 10 text messages from Javiar. He didn't know that her phone was switched off. He had somehow managed to pick her bra up and was asking her to come and get the bra once all his friends left. Maohi texted to enquire if they had left. She was almost convinced that he would have slept by now but his status changed from "offline"

The girl in a pink bow

to *"typing…"* immediately. He sent a photo of her bra next to him in his bed. "Unless you are being naughty, you need to put this back on". She giggled a little and the next thing she knew she was in the lift on her way to Javiar's penthouse.

There were 2 girls sitting on the couch and a couple was in the balcony. They were all a little too engrossed into each to notice maohi.

Javiar took Maohi's hand and made her follow him up the stairs and into his room. His room was neat and clean. Where there was a spread of alcohol on top of a white cloth, now there was a mint green bed sheet tucked in neatly. The room smelt of aftershave. His room had a private balcony that had the view of the city beyond the campus. He gave her a glass of water and added some electrolytes to it. He made one for himself as well. Though the lake water was fairly clean, it was still necessary to bathe and get rid of it. Javiar had bathed and changed into a fresh satin night suit. It was a satin cord set of pyjama bottoms and a buttoned half-sleeve shirt in dark gray. Maohi hadn't had the time to bathe, he undressed her after she finished her electrolytes and sent her to the bathroom with a smack on her bum for a quick shower. He set out a fresh cotton white t-shirt and blue checkered boxers for her.

Javiar's bathroom had limited products. There were 2 shower gels, a shampoo and a hair mask. She reached out for one of the shower gels, DIOR Sauvage. The other bottle looked fancier, so she kept his DIOR back and picked the pink bottle. It was L'Occitane Rose. She was happy to find a feminine shower gel but just when she was about to squirt some to soap her body, the image of Javiar showering with the 2 girls she saw on the couch flashed in her mind. She began to wonder if a girl had left or forgotten her body-wash or if he had purchased one for when he entertained girls in his bathroom because he clearly liked them clean. She pushed that image out of her head and began to clean her body as fast as she could. She was curious to see what direction the night would take. After cleaning her body, she picked a bottle of Kerastase to clean her hair. She decided to avoid the hair mask since she was in a hurry to step out. She had left her bathroom door open but shower curtains were drawn. Javiar had stepped in to let her know that he was hanging a fresh towel on the towel hanger for her. She picked up the towel and dried her body. She dried her hair and eventually draped herself in Versace, I <3 Baroque Bath Towel. It was in PINK! It wasn't his towel, he had one in blue hanging behind the door. The thought of other girls parading in and out of his bathroom re-entered Maohi's brain. It suddenly felt too crowded inside, she felt as if she was stacked and stuffed in one bathroom with millions of other girls, wrapped in pink. She tried to push her arms out as she started to get claustrophobic and ran towards the door to get out of the chaos. She stumbled out of the door in haste and dropped her towel. Javair said, "Were you being chased by someone in the bathroom, mama ceta?" Maohi composed herself and gave an awkward but proud smile. "I was just hurrying to get to you." She tried to flirt but failed miserably. Javaiar laughed very loudly at her attempt. He was used to a smart mouth running on a cute face while clumsily banging into things. Maohi trying to be enticing was an awkwardly funny site.

The girl in a pink bow

Javiar asked her if she had eaten anything all night. Maohi had not eaten because she had been consumed by her final submissions and then by Javiar. She had been on a liquid diet, coffee and alcohol, all day. He asked her to change into the clean clothes that he had set out for her while he got her something to eat. He dropped her bra on top of the pile of her dirty clothes. He shut the door behind him and instructed her to latch it. The elements loitering in the penthouse werent to be trusted. She obeyed as instructed. Maohi was glad that she was at least changing into his clothes and not some girl's. She was not even willing to entertain the thought of how many girls he had lent his clothes to. Javiar brought her a pizza and a taco with some Diet Coke. He played Bridgerton's first season for her while they ate. After washing down her shrimp taco with diet coke. She looked at him and asked him, "What is happening between us tonight?" He said, "Something that I had been dreaming about for a while but never had the courage to initiate". Javiar didn't want to spoil what they had in case Maohi did not approve of this. Now that both of them were taking summer off, he knew he was going to lose whatever they had shared over the past 4 months. He said that he wanted to spend the summer either getting over her or as her boyfriend. Maohi almost spilled her Diet Coke.

Maohi told him that because he flirted with all the other girls all the time in front of her, she never thought that he was ever into her. He explained that he had always been flirtatious and that's just who he is. Not flirting with Maohi was the biggest sign that she should have caught on to. He wanted to romance her. For Javiar, romancing a love interest was insanely

The girl in a pink bow

difficult, unlike flirting with a random stranger. He told Maohi that he had no energy to express what he felt and the things that he has been wanting to communicate for a while. He paused Bridgerton and they started to make out.

Chapter 22

Maohi kept replaying her interaction with Javiar in the last 4 months. She had first seen him in her Strategy class. They were being taught about how to make Business sense of scalability with an example of whether to invest in a new production unit based on the current demand and operational cost. Javiar was the first one to raise his hand. Since he came from the world of fashion, his question was about how you factor the intrinsic value attached to a brand. Any brand that sold clothes in Walmart could factor the scalability mostly on the extrinsic values but how would a brand like LVMH gauge the intrinsic value of its products to project scalability calculations? Maohi was fascinated by his curiosity for intangible aspects of life. She believed that life existed in the intangible and since different people attach different values to them and it keeps on varying throughout their lives, that is why it's very difficult to ever make sense of this world.

We all interact in a given space and time as we consume the resources, while desperately trying to make sense of it all. We begin by trying to control it, and when we fail at that, we try and make sense of it. Once we realise how arbitrary human interactions are, that's when it's best to internalise our experience to evaluate what works best for us. We need to reach a point in life where we learn to accept our external environment as is and be self-aware to fit ourselves where we fit best. It's a lifelong journey of identifying what's best for us and there is no guarantee that what's best for us today would also be best for us tomorrow.

By the time the first week of her 3rd semester had ended, she was happy to have Javiar in 4 of her classes. She was hoping to have him as one of her teammates in at least one of the first group assignments from all 4 subjects. Luckily for her, Javiar was her partner in their first Operations Project. It was a 2-team project where they had to design a sushi conveyor belt at a restaurant.

Assignment - 3 chefs, 1 cleaner. The sushi belt stays in the kitchen for 1/4th of its length and 3/4th of it is in the restaurant.

Find the best way to serve the customers seated around the belt.

Maohi and Javiar connected over WhatsApp and decided to meet in the library to solve it. Maohi had been waiting for him for 15 minutes and Javiar was "fashionably" late. He was wearing a lavender Beanie, a Lavender down coat, blue jeans and black snow boots. It snowed almost every day in the month

The girl in a pink bow

of Jan. He apologised for being late as he removed his coat to reveal a baby pink cashmere. Maohi had no idea at this point that he was a fashion designer, she felt extremely underdressed in her white hoodie and her black woollen jeggings. Her navy blue Decathlon boots with fur were her saving grace in front of this Fancy Diva. Maohi was hoping that her Fluorescent pink down jacket was on. But it was too hot in the library.

They greeted each other and immediately got to work. They both had a lecture in an hour. They made a list of things to be discussed. First topic was if each chef should prepare the entire plate (Job Shop) or should they have each do one task on the conveyor belt (Flow shop/Assembly Line) directly - The 1st chef places the sushi roll and its filling on the plate, the second rolls it into a neat roll and the 3rd cuts it into 4 pieces. Or if one chef should be working off the conveyor belt and only 2 should be working on it. They explored various permutations and combinations along with strategizing the speed of the belt and the area and time to be allotted to the chefs and the cleaner on the conveyor belt. They also discussed assumptions like if any particular cook was pro at any part of the sushi making activity, would one activity all day make it very monotonous for the cook? Etc. Maohi was impressed by the ideas and the practical aspects that Javiar was bringing in. Before they knew it, one hour was up. They had set an alarm for a hard stop and the moment it rang, Javiar asked Maohi if she would like to accompany him on his coffee run. They got some coffee and a cookie each and attended their last lecture for the day from the library.

The girl in a pink bow

They decided to get something to eat after their lecture. That's how Maohi and Javiar spent their first day/date together. Maohi had been very excited about meeting a charming boy and she was smitten by his brains too. He was absolutely casual and comfortable. Maohi loved his sense of humor, which only got better towards the end of the day. Mehul was Maohi's partner for her coffee runs on her free days and Javiar on the days they had the same lectures. From that day onwards, they attended most of their lectures together. There were times when they would be confined in Maohi's room, and she would feel some sexual tension between them, but she always distanced herself in those moments, worrying that he might think of her as a creep.

Now, laying next to him in his bed while he was fast asleep. She wondered if all those times it wasn't just her feeling the tingling in the pit of her stomach. Every time she awkwardly tried to put some space or distance between them, he grunted hoarsely under his breath.

She kept worrying if all he wanted was a night of passion before they parted ways, now that the semester had ended. She kept telling herself that if that was the case, then she would be grateful for tonight and the friendship that they had shared in the past 4 months. But she would not go ahead and have a one night stand. She knew in her heart that after sharing this intimacy, she would not be able to go back to being friends.

If he was going to be an active presence in her life, then she would want more. In the hope of wanting more or feeling more, she might end up giving into more such intimate nights, which would further make her feelings towards Javair stronger. She knew if she didn't pull away, she would fall into this vicious cycle. Just like every other time, she would try to convince herself that she was making the most of what life was throwing at her or tell herself that Javiar was a phase and she would get over it. But this time, she knew she couldn't afford to be stupid. Because she admired Javiar, she was fond of him and news flash, she had fallen for him. Harder than she could have ever imagined. She knew that if he wasn't willing to give more, she would have to cut all ties.

The thought of not being able to see Javiar ever again made her sob. Javiar flinched a little in his sleep because of the sobbing noise. He didn't wake up but hugged her tighter. Maohi hoped to get some sleep since she couldn't move anyway. At that moment, she thought, though being loved and being embraced by a charming boy is every girl's dream, sometimes all you need is a little space. All she wanted to do at that moment was to get a cup of coffee with a cigarette and to be on her own balcony by herself. But instead, she was trying not to move so she attempted to get some shut eye. There was barely any time left for sunrise.

She woke up to a clink of cutlery. Javiar had brought her breakfast in bed. Sunny side up on sourdough with some bacon and hash browns on the side and a glass of cold orange juice with pulp. They sat and ate their meal in the bedroom and then he got her some blueberry pancakes with her coffee, and they took the rest of their breakfast to the balcony. Maohi barely ate anything and by now, was grabbing onto her coffee mug as if it were her life raft. She knew it was time for Javiar to speak about his feelings.

The girl in a pink bow

Javiar had always been very expressive and vocal about his feelings. He had discussed his family issues and the setbacks he had to face in his business and how it made him feel. He was very grateful to be able to finance his current education on his own, at one point, he had stopped dreaming about it, but eventually he managed to follow through.

Though he had never complimented Maohi, he was very vocal about sexualising women. Sexualising anyone has a very bad connotation to it because it's interpreted as looking at someone as a sex object. But the problem should ideally be with objectification as is. We as a society categorise men as "husband material" based on their ability to provide and highly domestic women are branded as "wife material". This objectification isn't based on the way they look but on the features that they come with and the services that they can offer..

Since Javiar never showed any admiration towards Maohi, she assumed that he enjoyed her company and that was all there was to it. Javiar hadn't initiated more the previous night either. Maohi had imagined every possibility in the last 12 hours, from thinking that all he wanted was one night of passion but didn't go all the way because she was bad in bed to shortlisting her wedding couture.

Maohi sipped her coffee one more time before she asked him about the night that they had spent together. "Did you want to be with me just once because you were curious?.. Or…". Javiar cut her mid-sentence, "I have loved you from the day I saw you in the library". Maohi was not ready for the "L" word. Never could she have ever anticipated that Javiar would tell her that he loved her. Maohi tightened her grip on the mug as if that

The girl in a pink bow

was the only thing keeping her from getting tossed off and drowning into the depths of his sincerity. She had had a crush on him and she knew that he was aware of it. Almost every girl who was an active participant in his life had a minor crush on him. He regularly met with models, outside the university, to discuss his work. Even though he was a full-time student, he could not afford to completely detach from his work for 2 years. All these models were always puppy-eyed around him and he enjoyed the importance.

Chapter- 23

Maohi had so many questions. She thought that he was casually dating multiple women and getting laid on a regular basis. "Never have I ever casually dated; I only get involved when there is love. Maohi, I would be lying if I said that I haven't had sex in the last 4 months," Javiar accepted. He spoke about one drunken night with an old flame. He was meeting this girl in Downtown for a few drinks. She was his crush, but they had never dated. He got too drunk and couldn't return to the campus, so she offered to host him and they ended up having sex. Javiar told her that he didn't feel guilty about any of it because it was a one-time thing and even though he had eyes only for Maohi but they weren't in a relationship yet. "You could love one person and choose to indulge with others as long as you have not voluntarily taken up the responsibility of never breaking their heart". He gave into his sexual urges that night.

Javiar had a lot at stake and he was very committed towards his course. Attending lectures with Maohi was reflecting positively on his grades and he didn't want to do anything to jinx it. He had decided not to express his feelings until the last day of their semester. Javiar said that he didn't want Maohi to leave his side even for a minute last night. He had kept his desires in check for a quarter of a year. Finally, he didn't have to pretend anymore, so he wanted her by himself. The hour that she spent with her batchmates at the lake was very irritating for Javiar.

"Javiar, this is a lot to digest. I have always had a crush on you, but I kept myself from falling for you. I couldn't have imagined even in the wildest of my dreams that you would ever love me. You masked it fantastically."

Javiar told her that he had kept himself under a check for the sake of their professional life. Both Maohi and Javiar were progressive and believed in achieving their dreams. He admired her obedience and commitment towards her dreams and he knew she had the aptitude to fulfil all her desires. She was grateful and impressed with his maturity. He made sure that they extracted the best that they could out of their friendship, academically. Without bringing in any romantic or sexual distractions.

Both Javiar and Maohi had taken up internships during summer. Since the office spaces had restricted the number of employees, both of them had hybrid mode. They were to work from Monday to Thursday. Maohi had to go to the office on Tuesdays and Wednesdays and Javiar had Mondays and

The girl in a pink bow

Wednesdays. It was Saturday morning, and their internships were starting the following week on Thursday.

Javiar had planned a getaway for the two of them, he had been planning it for the last one month. He had booked a room in one of the fanciest hotels, adjacent to a vineyard in Niagara on the Lake, and he had booked various wine tastings. They were to head out today and spend the night at Niagara Falls and head to Niagara on the lake on Sunday."Maohi, please come with me to Niagara. I want to give us a fair chance". Maohi knew that she would regret not going on this trip, irrespective of how things turned out.

Maohi had tried to refrain from entertaining the idea of getting romantically or sexually involved with Javiar but had been failing miserably in her attempt. She knew that she had a lot at stake if she started to foster her admiration towards Javiar. She had never let herself fantasize about him in any capacity. Though the thought of it kept entering her mind but she had to keep pushing it out.

One night, they had booked the last slot for their swim. The last slot sometimes gave them extra time if the coach was lenient about the closing time. The Coach himself came in for a dip before closing the health club. The LifeGuard blew his whistle and asked the 3 of us to step out. The Lifeguard handed over the keys of the health club to the Coach. Maohi and Javiar were drinking water and collecting their belongings that they had placed by the pool. There was no one around the pool now, and Javiar told Maohi that he had always accessed the girl's locker room all his life. He hadn't done that here so far. Before Maohi could stop him, he had already sneaked in. As he was

The girl in a pink bow

exploring the area, a lady came to check up on Maohi. The coach thought that Javiar left directly from the pool and he had sent someone from the cleaning staff to ensure that Maohi had left. Maohi and Javiar jumped into a cramped-up shower space when the lady came enquiring. Maohi turned on the shower and pretended to bathe and asked the lady to give her 5 minutes. Javiar whispered in her ears, "Let's shampoo and soap our bodies, now that we are here.". They both dressed up and left the locker room. He sneaked out behind her. Every time Maohi thought about that shower, she got turned on.

Now, the thought of spending 3 days with him, away from everyone else in a romantic place, was absolutely enticing. It had been 2 minutes since Javiar had invited her for a getaway, and Maohi hadn't uttered a word yet. "Yaa, now would be a good time to not to respond," Javiar joked sarcastically. " I am getting jittery. It could be the coffee, but the chances are that it's the anticipation of your response". Maohi snapped out of her thought process, and before Javair could ask again, she got up and told him that she would meet him at the building entrance in 2 hours. She didn't want to waste any more time not being on this fantasy trip.

Chapter 24

Maohi rushed to her apartment in his clothes and that's when she ran into Suvreen. Now, they were both sitting on their balcony. Suvreen was listening to Maohi's shenanigans intently. She gave Maohi a list of chocolates that she wanted and also asked her to get a bottle of wine from the vineyard. Maohi plugged in her phone before she jumped in for her shower. She was out within 5 minutes and she packed her bag, naked. She didn't want to waste any time. She packed her lacy Victoria's Secrets and her sexiest night suits. She packed 4 summer dresses and 3 evening dresses, 2 pairs of shorts, cotton and denim each and 4 cotton t-shirts. While packing, she was taken back to the only time she had dressed up fancy in Canada. It was during her quarantine with Leonardo. She was contemplating packing the pink co ord set that she had worn the first time they shared their meal and at that moment, her phone buzzed. Coincidentally, it was Leonardo! He hadn't texted her after their Quarantine. They occasionally reacted to each other's stories on Insta but that was all about it.

An Instagram notification flashed on her locked screen.

LeoNArtDuo - Congratulations!

Maohi and her batchmates had posted and tagged each other in multiple stories since last night. All the stories had a common theme - semester completion. Maohi didn't open the text message. She had no time to entertain this confusion. She decided against packing the co ord set. She wore a navy blue printed chiffon divided skirt and a white tube crop top. She wore her sports shoes and packed 2 pairs of heels and a pair of flats. Javiar called her just before she was about to tie her shoelaces. He wanted to check if he could book a cab to the Union station. They decided to meet at the building entrance in 5 minutes.

They reached Union station at 11 AM, and their train to Niagara was at 11:30 AM. Maohi hadn't had the chance to enjoy her coffee, she was busy first with Javiar and then narrating everything to Suvreen. Before she could say anything, Leonardo was already standing in line at Starbucks to get her her coffee. He brought 2 hot Hazelnut Lattes with whipped cream and caramel drizzle and they walked towards the platform from where they had to board. It was fairly less crowded for a Saturday, they found a bench to sit on and drink their coffee.

A double-decker train arrived at their platform. They both took their seats on the second deck. The seats were facing each other, and there was a huge window and the train had a glass roof. The upper deck was filled with natural sunlight. Maohi's

The girl in a pink bow

pupils were dilated like a 5-year-old's. It had been a while since she had felt this feeling of belonging. It had been 3 years since Aleb and Maohi had ended things. Though the official breakup happened later, the process had commenced around this time 3 years ago. She hadn't had a boyfriend who brought her Starbucks and held her hand while she sipped her coffee. Javiar rested his head on Maohi and both of them enjoyed the view. They kissed on lips not more than once or twice but Javiar kept holding her hands and kissing them every 10-15 minutes.

They got down at their station and booked a cab to the falls from the station. Both of them were visiting it for the first time, and they found it mesmerizing. There was so much moisture in and around that area that there were multiple tiny rainbows suspended around it. None of them were interested in taking the boat ride, so they decided to explore the souvenir shop. They walked around and reached the postcards section. The salesman there told them that they could buy postcards and collect stamps from the checkout counter. There was a postbox just after the exit. Maohi and Javiar each bought postcards to send to their families. Maohi had never sent a postcard in her life, this was her first time. Javiar had sent it once before, but that was on a school trip, and it was one of the activities that was part of the trip. Maohi picked 2 postcards, one for her dad and one for her mom. One postcard changed the image when you changed the angle, lenticular printing. One photo was of the colorful lights that fall on the Niagara Falls at night, and the other one was a day picture with a rainbow. She addressed that to her father. The other postcard was a picture of the falls from the boat ride, as close as one could be under the falls in the

The girl in a pink bow

water. It looked magnificent in the postcard, and she addressed this to her mother. Javiar bought only one, the second one, that he addressed to both his parents.

Hello Mama

I miss you, I love you.

Hope to see you soon.

Love Maohi

Hello Papa

I missed you when I crossed the casinos on my way to the waterfall from the railway station.

Take care

Love Maohi

Hola Mom dad

I miss you both every day!

I hope I get home before this postcard does. 😁

Love Javiar.

Maohi had no Idea that Javiar was planning to visit Mexico this summer. She wanted to ask him but she decided otherwise. Maohi didn't want to worry about what part of the summer she would be spending without him, nor could she ask him not to go, at least not yet. But she also felt that it would be unfair if he planned to spend more than 2 weeks back home.

Maohi picked a pink Envelope for her mother and a blue one for her dad and Javiar picked a pink one. They sealed it and stuck the stamps on them. They wrote their respective addresses and left the souvenir shop. They had to ask and navigate to the correct exit that had the red postbox. After 15 minutes of loitering in the mall, they finally saw it next to one of the exits, and they slid their envelopes into it. Javiar booked their cab to the hotel. The hotel was a surprise for Maohi; she had no idea about where he was taking her.

After a 5-minute cab ride, she got down in front of a huge building, and Javiar checked them into their penthouse. They entered the room, and he opened the curtains; the window had a view of the Falls. Both Maohi and Javiar were enchanted, like 10-year-olds, by the view. The porter left their room, and the moment they heard the click of the door, they started kissing. They made love all evening and then went out to get some dinner. By the time they got back to the hotel, they were too exhausted as they had barely slept in the last 48 hours. They slept as soon as they got into their bed.

Maohi and Javiar grabbed a quick breakfast the next day and were now on their way to their next destination. It was almost a 45-minute drive to "Cows", a very famous ice cream parlour that sold very cute merchandise as well. They got down there and Javiar took her for an ice cream. The layout of the outlet was such that you had to cross all the cute vibrant merchandise. Maohi saw a very cute pair of socks. She bought a pink and a black colour socks that had the face of their signature cow on it.

Maohi got herself 2 scoops of Gooey Mooey. As soon as they got out of the shop. Javiar took out a piece of Lavender satin cloth to blindfold Maohi. He had planned the ice cream

The girl in a pink bow

to keep her entertained while she was blindfolded on their way to the hotel. It was another 10-minute cab ride away. He had asked the hotel to pick them up from a pickup point that was 2-3 minutes walking distance from the ice cream parlour. The street was very crowded, and Maohi was skeptical about his plan. She looked around at the crowd and then at Javiar. "Yea, I guess I didn't think this through and never have I ever done it, but I am going to try it anyway", Javiar said. Maohi thought what was the worst that could happen, she wanted to be a sport. No one had ever made Maohi feel so special; hence, even with all the apprehensions, she was excited about going through with it. Maohi handed over her luggage to Javiar and helped him set both their bags in a way that he could drag them all with one hand so his one hand was free to guide Maohi.

After tying the cloth on her eyes, Javiar took a bite from her ice cream and started to guide her. He was holding her hand and guiding her, people around them started to make way for them, she heard an occasional "aawwww....". Most of them had seen this happen only in movies. Maohi asked Javiar if they were attracting attention, and he told her that people were looking at him with admiration for such a romantic gesture. "I deserve an extra kiss". Maohi blurted out the word extra and turned towards him, or at least where she thought he was. But he had changed sides to avoid a pole. Maohi banged into that pole as she turned while exclaiming, "EXTRA!" there was no room for extra. Javiar speaking of it so casually threw her off balance, figuratively and literally. He saved the ice cream from hitting the pole. Maohi felt his hand on her hands and realised that he chose to save the ice cream.

"Priorities! Are you saving the ice cream?", Maohi taunted. "In my defence, that's all I could save, so I did", Javiar responded. Maohi felt her forehead for a bump, luckily, there was none. They continued their walk to the cab. Javiar stopped to look for their car. He looked around and spotted it. The car had the hotel's name written all over it.

Javiar was sure that Maohi had heard the name of the hotel because though most of the students never booked a room there, whoever went to Niagara at least visited the property. Mikhail had visited the property once with one of his bumble dates, he was telling his experience of the property. The awe with which Maohi was listening to Mikhail's experience urged Javiar to put the hotel on his "Things to do with Maohi" list.

Javiar made Maohi wait at some distance from the cab. He went up to the cab driver and explained the situation to him. He told him that at any point during their conversation if he felt the need to use the name of the hotel, he must swap its name with "Artichoke".

Either the cabby was very talkative, or he had stumbled on something entertaining on a regular day of his mundane job. He used the word artichoke at least 15 times in their 10-minute ride. After the 10th time, Maohi's curiosity had peaked, and she said, "As you can clearly see that my vision is compromised, could you please confirm if the hotel that I am being driven to is called Artichoke?" The driver looked in the rearview mirror and raised an eyebrow at Javiar, and Javiar nodded a yes. Cabby obeyed and continued to talk about Artichoke.

Chapter- 25

Maohi was standing outside a huge castle. There was a white picket fence, circumfrencing the lawns on all four sides. A huge mansion stood in the centre of the lawns. The cab had dropped them in front of the entrance. They entered through a wooden gate; it had an old rusting look and was covered in grapevine. There were plum coloured Tulips planted on each side of the Cobblestone pathway that lead to the door of the mansion. Maohi felt like a princess, clumsily and inappropriately dressed, gliding towards it. Javiar was right behind her, carrying all of their luggage. Maohi had forgotten about him for a moment. The minute she looked behind, he looked equally enchanted as he absorbed his surroundings while dragging their bags. Maohi ran towards Javiar and hugged him tightly. She kissed him and thanked him for the beautiful surprise.

The girl in a pink bow

As they started to approach the mansion, Maohi could finally tell they had reached "Le Paradis". It was the fanciest hotel she had ever heard of.

There was a porter at the gate waiting to collect and scan their luggage. They handed over their bags to him and entered. The interiors were of white marble and champagne colored carvings and edges. It had wooden furniture with couches and cushions of chocolate brown leather. The same plum Tulips were used to decorate the entire entrance. There must have been at least 100 of them in and around the reception/lobby area. The aesthetics were gorgeous. Maohi felt a little underdressed, but she was grateful that she had packed enough dresses. She nudged Javiar towards her.

Maohi - "I am extremely underdressed. I am not even appropriately dressed to be serving the housekeeping here. I feel the need to pull the tray of refreshments from them and apologise because they have to serve me."

Javiar - "Sweetheart, I promise on any other day I would have said that you could never look anything but an epitome of poise irrespective of your clothes. But today, I am going to agree with you. I did a thorough research and was proud of myself to dress in something casually fancy. But I have put myself to shame as a fashion designer."

They went to check in, and he told the concierge that he had booked a premier room, the one with the view of the vineyard and the grape vines. The concierge asked for the booking number. Javiar gave the booking ID: "The booking ID is 04112023". The concierge's expression changed as he

The girl in a pink bow

frantically moved the mouse to click all over his computer screen. Javiar could tell that there was a problem; he started to panic, and it elevated with every click of the mouse. Javiar reached out to his phone to check for the booking details; by now, he was sure that he had goofed up. Maohi reached out to hold his hand, the one that was reaching for his mobile. She looked at him with a look of reassurance and smiled. Javiar relaxed immediately and smiled back at her.

When Javiar was reaching for his phone in his pocket, he had imagined Maohi's face to be sadly quizzical. He was in self-doubt; he had no courage to look into her eyes. Until he was sure that he had made the correct booking, he wasn't going to have the courage to meet her eyes. But the moment she took his hand and smiled at him instead, he felt that he had entered a new world. In this world, the woman that he adored had the magical powers to give life a happy twist, irrespective of the situation. Just through the positivity that she put out in the world. Something inside of him changed, and he had never felt so grateful and content. It was a transcending experience.

The concierge looked up from his system and towards the couple. "I apologise, but there is a small problem. The guests that occupied the room that you had requested were supposed to check out today but they decided to extend their stay with us. However, I can offer you an upgrade, the view will be that of the lake. If you would be willing to compromise on the grapes and embrace water, I have a fabulous suite for you". Their faces immediately lit back up.

On the right-hand side was a huge staircase, imitating the one in Titanic where Jack's eyes fill with love when he sees Rose walking down. On the other end were 2 elevators. It was a 5-floor atrium, including the ground floor, with a glass ceiling. The ground floor had the dining room, breakfast area that extended to an outdoor pool side area, Heated pool and jacuzzi next to a gymnasium. These were a few things that Maohi could see as she loitered around in the lobby. There were 20 rooms on the first 3 floors, and the 4th floor had 6 suites. You could see all the floors from the lobby, and the roof on top was all glass. Natural light enhanced the aesthetics.

Maohi decided to take the stairs. Javiar took the elevator with the porter and their luggage. Unlike the ground floor, which had white marble on the floor, the staircase and the corridors leading to rooms were carpeted in chocolate brown plush. The golden thread weaved in the carpet sparkled under the sunlight. The 1st and 2nd floor had regular rooms and the 3rd floor had premium rooms. The stairway that led to the Suites needed the keycard to access it. She had to call Javiar to come and get her.

Though Maohi was active, she wasn't at her fittest. She was out of breath by the time she reached the 3rd floor. She was glad that she would be able to catch some breath and she wouldn't have to climb another floor, else she would have been panting miserably by the time she got to her room. Breathless Maohi would have been a little embarrassed in front of Javiar. He regularly played soccer right before his swim sessions with Maohi, and his stamina and fitness levels were incredible. Maohi had caught her breath by the time she heard the access door to the 4th floor click.

Javiar: "Shrek came here to save his princess trapped in the tower, but today he would only be saving the donkey on the staircase."

Maohi: "Mean"

Javiar: "Sorry, babe! Firstly, it's an insult to this place if I called you a princess in this attire. Secondly, you need the wits of a donkey to get stuck on the staircase."

Javiar was cocky and Maohi had the appetite to take jokes.

Dating apps have made it easier. The times when friendships were almost inevitable, before romance bloomed, were better. Friendships give you the required access to understand someone. People meet on dating apps and judge each other through their social media accounts. Our instagrams, facebooks, Orkuts, snapchats, Twitters, etc... Even LinkedIn is just a reflection of our best parts. There is more to us than what these apps project; most of us are not self-aware enough to be able to project our thoughts and feelings accurately. The ugly gets missed out and resurfaces later in the relationships. People need to connect organically and spend some time with each other before they interact with each other's virtual facades. There isn't so much perfection in the world that social media helps us in projecting. Consumption of the perfect world on social media has decreased our tolerance to imperfections.

Fortunately for Javiar and Maohi, they had spent 4 months being friends. They had been through intense deadlines and pool splashes. They had had their fair share of physical interactions to build a meaningful bond. They were fortunate enough to have had the chance to know each other outside the virtual world.

Chapter - 26

The moment Maohi set foot on the 5th floor, it felt like she had walked into heaven. The floor was made of powder pink marble. Chunks of irregularly shaped glittering rose gold stones were embedded into it. The railing, door handles, wall lamps and all other metal fixtures were glittering rose gold. All the lampshades were pastel pink. Maohi felt like she was on cloud 9, quite literally. Javiar felt proud when he saw the look on Maohi's face. He had finally achieved the look that he was hoping to see on her. She looked so pretty walking towards their suite in the natural light that he wanted to cease this moment and capture it forever. At that moment, he knew he wanted to spend the rest of his life with her.

The staircase led to suite 508, and they took a left to get to their suite, 510. Suite 512 was right across the elevator. Maohi stood in front of an open door wide-eyed; Javiar could swear that he saw the entire universe twinkling in her once again dilated pupils. He didn't anticipate the extent of elation Maohi exuded. Javiar didn't know that bodies could convey such elaborate emotions. Though he hadn't seen the suite yet, more than the suite, he was now looking forward to experiencing Maohi's expressive body language and expressions when she stepped into the suite.

They entered into a beautifully sunlit apartment. The glass ceiling was extended into their room. The flooring and the metal fixtures were identical to what they saw in the corridor. There were 2 huge and cozy couches facing the fireplace in one corner of the living room. The living area opened into a cute balcony overlooking the vineyard. The balcony had a breakfast table with 4 chairs, 2 sunbeds and a jacuzzi hot tub. The wall opposite the fireplace had huge windows that had a view of the lake. Every piece of furniture was eggshell with pastel pink cushions, throws, etc. The door on the opposite end from the balcony opened into the room. The glass ceiling on top of the bed tapered into a slant. The room had a view of the water as well. The bathroom was just like another glass-covered balcony. It had a huge showerhead installed in the glass ceiling. There was a vanity mirror and a counter opposite to the shower, which had an open roof.

Maohi and Javiar were in awe of the suite, so much so that they had forgotten about the porter waiting with their luggage at the door. They stepped out into the living area and instructed him to bring in all the luggage. He informed them about the different sections of the suite and the functionalities. The glass windows had blinds, the ceiling had a shutter that they could slide shut to block the natural light. Javiar walked the porter out while enquiring about the stock in the mini bar and the fridge. Maohi was least interested in noting any more information.

From the moment Javiar had blind folded her, she had started to give into his lead. She was slowly settling into her feminine energy.

Maohi had been hustling for over 5 years. She had been pushing her limits to ensure she would never have to depend on anyone in any capacity. She was always in control and self-sufficient. But the last 2 days with Javiar were something else. He was bossy and controlling and none of it was for his own selfish interest. He had been nothing but thoughtful. By now, Maohi's brain had started to obey, and her body was submitting to him. She was enjoying letting go of the control without having to second-guess if the instructions would be in her best interest.

She entered their bedroom, the bed was inviting. She just wanted to strip and get inside the sheets. Maohi started to strip and thought she would have some time before Javiar got done with the porter, but he entered before she could get into the bed.

He pulled her into the fancy bathroom for a hot water shower. After a few minutes, she realised that he was reaching for the body wash. She stepped back to get some for herself and they both cleaned themselves. Now that they had enjoyed each other, they were just two adults desperate to clean themselves and dry their bodies to slip into the world's most comfortable bed. Javiar finished first and kissed Maohi on her forehead before stepping out. Maohi stepped out of the bathroom after

The girl in a pink bow

5 minutes, wrapped in a white towel. Javiar, by then, had rolled down the blinds and closed the shutters. The room was pitch dark, and the AC was on full blast. Javiar handed Maohi one of his favourite night suits of her. She didn't know that he had a favourite until today.

One night, he had come to borrow 2 eggs from Maohi, and she was wearing the same night suit. That was the first time Javiar noticed Maohi. It was late in the night, and she wasn't wearing anything under her white strapless bandeau. That was the first time he couldnt stop thinking pf her. She put on her shorts and strapless bandeau, and they slipped under the sheets. They spooned for 2 minutes tops before they drifted into a sound sleep. They wanted to look their best for the wine tasting.

Chapter- 27

Maohi and Javiar entered the dining room. It was a huge room with almost 100 tables. Each table had a floral arrangement of Tulips. Every table had the number of the room displayed next to the centrepiece, and as they approached their table, there were name cards of every guest in front of the chair.

Maohi was wearing a short, white tube dress. She looked like a dark-haired tinkerbell but in white. Her lips were blood red and the blush on her cheeks twinned with the pink of the tulips in the centrepiece. She batted her eyes at Javiar from time to time because she was proud of the perfection with which she winged her eyes, and the nude eyeshadow complimented it perfectly. She was desperately waiting to be seated at her table because her gold pumps were too high for her comfort.

Javiar was dressed in a white linen shirt, buttoned down to bare a significant portion of his chest. He wore beige khakis, long enough to just touch his ankles. He paired his outfit with gray loafers. He had neatly tucked his hair back with a little moose. He pulled the chair for Maohi, and she was relieved to be seated. A few guests were already seated, a few were still walking in. Servers were carrying different wines to be served to the table, each table had a charcuterie board. There was a separate plate for different kinds of cheese and there were small portions of meals being served to compliment the wines.

The moment Javiar was seated, a server approached their table with their charcuterie board and the additional plate of cheese. He gave a detailed description of their welcome snack. Once he was finished, he said "I will be serving you tonight. my name is Mathew. I will be following the flow of wines that the hotel has curated".

The hotel hosted this dinner every night. The guests who had checked in the same day were seated close to each other with different servers. These servers were to give them a detailed explanation of the wines because they were to pick and choose the wine tour that they would like to go on the next day. To give their guests a fulfilling experience, the hotel curated different wine tours at different times and hosted a meal after the tour.

The server started with white wine, followed by rose and then red.

They were served 4 variants under each category and a small bite to go with each. During the process, the servers kept requesting them to eat a cracker or white bread from the charcuterie board to cleanse their palates. He also explained the importance of a palate cleanser in wine tasting. Mathew said, "To be sensitive to different notes of ingredients in the wine, it's important to reset your palate. A lingering note of cherry in the mouth might interfere with the next glass of red." There were different ways of twirling, clockwise and anticlockwise. Every sip could taste different based on how you were handling your wine. The servers were in no rush, and they let the guests savour their experience. If any guest liked some wine and wanted to have a glass of it, they could order one before their next round of tasting. The only constraint was that all the guests at one table had to decide if they wanted to pause or continue. Different guests at the same table could not pause the wine tasting at different times.

Javiar said, "Let's order our top 2 wines after every round of tasting" Maohi agreed "I get to pick the top 2 for white wine and you can do the same for red, for rose we can pick one each." Maohi liked Charoday the most, she ordered one glass of Chardonnay and one of Pinot Grigio - her second favourite of the four they had just tasted. They ordered a plate of steamed fish in butter garlic sauce with mashed potatoes with their wines.

Javiar excused himself to go to the restroom. Maohi realised she hadn't checked her messages since yesterday. The last thing she had seen was an Instagram notification from Leonardo, congratulating her. She unlocked her phone and started to scroll through Instagram. She realised she had barely taken any pictures to post on Insta. She eventually opened her messages. Everyone was curious about Maohi being unavailable. All her batchmates had texted her, asking about her whereabouts. She

The girl in a pink bow

informed everyone and shared her location with Suvreen and her other WhatsApp group. She finally reached Leonardo's text, she thanked him.

She was happy with Javiar, even though she didn't know where all this was headed, but she didn't want to taint the experience with any confusing emotions. Maohi switched from Leo's message to her Insta feed. She was going through the stories of her friends and most of her feed was filled with random stories of their final submission night. Everyone was celebrating finishing their winter term and welcoming summer. While she was flipping through the stories, she suddenly breathed in the best mixture of masculine with a Louis Vuitton Meteore. Before she could recover from the fragrance of hell and heaven combined, she felt the softest lips on her forehead. "I am back, sweetcheeks". Javiar looked enticing and loaded with cuteness.

Javiar was walking towards his table from the little men's room. He saw Maohi sitting on the table, she had pulled her hair together in a ponytail with a pink bow. Javiar could never imagine how beautiful Maohi was. Today was the first time that she had dolled up. He had only seen her dressed very casually and with some lip gloss and a pair of cat eye specs. When she got dressed tonight to step out for dinner. Javiar was avoiding looking at her because he was mesmerised by her beauty and he was too embarrassed to let Maohi find out what effect her beauty was having on him. Now, she was engrossed in her phone and completely ignorant of Javiar admiring her from a distance. He could take in all of her from a distance; he admired her for 5 minutes and then started to walk towards her. The

The girl in a pink bow

closer he got, the prettier she looked. The moment he reached their table, he leaned in to kiss her forehead before he took his seat.

The wine was served with the fish; they clinked and toasted to happiness. The food was the best they had ever tasted, the ambience was grand, and their hearts were warm. At this point, both of them were two happy kids in an amusement park with their best friend. The conversations were not romantic, they were not flirting or trying to impress each other. Both of them sat there, secure and comfortable with each other, discussing what all should they be exploring in the next 2 days.

Javiar had finished his glass of wine, and the server reached out to check if he wanted a refill. Javiar and Maohi decided to get back to their wine tasting, rose was next. They again ordered a glass of rose each and decided to sample their cheese platter with it.

Javiar ordered a glass of Merlot and a glass of Shiraz to go with their steak. By the time their food was being prepared, a server was helping them to decide on the wine tour that they would like to go on the following day. Both of them decided on a white wine tour. He told them that they would have to report at 11 AM at the reception. The food arrived as soon as the booking formalities finished. They enjoyed their steak and drank their wine. They shared their food and glasses of wine throughout the evening.

They got into their rooms, undressed themselves and went to bed. They were too sleepy and stuffed from the extravagant dinner. There was no room for any love-making or fooling around. They kissed each other goodnight and spooned. Maohi asked Javiar if he would like to join her for a swim in the morning, but there was no response because he had already slept off. Maohi pulled herself away from him to set her alarm for 7 AM. She wanted to work out for an hour before breakfast.

Maohi woke up and snoozed her alarm for 10 minutes. She turned around to look for Javiar but he wasn't there. She woke up and went to the living room. He was standing on the balcony, admiring the view with a glass of warm water with lemon and honey. She went back to her room, brushed her teeth and switched off her alarm. Maohi prepared herself the same infusion and joined Javiar on the balcony. She wanted to go for a swim but Javiar had to catch up with his work. He hadn't tended to his emails all day yesterday, so he needed some time by himself before breakfast.

Maohi had forgotten to pack her swimming costume, so she went to the hotel store. She bought herself an Orange swimsuit. The swimsuit was completely backless. If she put her hair down to cover the armhole strings, then anyone standing behind her would think she was walking around in her orange panties. The hotel had 2 pools, indoor and outdoor. Maohi preferred to swim in the sun, and the temperature outside was comfortable. The pool had a lawn next to it, and beyond the lawn was the lake. She borrowed a yoga mat and did a few rounds of surya namaskar next to the lake. After about 15 minutes, she decided to change into her swimsuit. After 15 non-stop laps of a 20-meter pool, she stopped for a 2-minute break and then did 15 more. By the time she got down with her second round, Javiar was standing by the pool and waiting for her. She untied her hair and stepped out from the opposite side. She wanted to tease Javiar and make him think that she had been swimming only in her bikini bottoms. The moment she picked up her towel and turned around. She got the expression she had been anticipating. She laughed and opened her towel. He was about to yell and ask her not to, but before he could, she exposed the front of her costume. He felt silly and laughed about it. Maohi went inside the changing rooms. She took a shower to remove all the chlorine from her body and her hair. She changed into white cotton shorts and an olive bralette.

Maohi left her hair open to air dry. She moisturised her face nicely to counter the dryness/skin damage from the chlorine and applied a cherry lip balm on her lips. Javiar was waiting for her in the breakfast area next to the pool. He took a place outdoors under an umbrella. Maohi looked equally pretty, without any makeup, if not prettier than yesterday. Javiar was baffled. He didn't know if it was the holiday glow or if he had fallen in love. He could swear that he had never thought of her to be such a beauty. He knew she was an attractive woman with a sharp mind and a kind heart. He was surrounded by models all the time in Mexico, so beauty wasn't a rarity. He had seen so much beauty in abundance that Maohi never stood out until today. She was very casually dressed, but for Javiar, she was the prettiest girl.

Maohi spotted Javiar on the breakfast table, his hair all messy and his eyes still a little sleepy; he had dozed off when he was on his second email. Anyone who saw Javiar and Maohi together felt that both of them complimented each other. They were a perfect couple, aesthetically speaking. They both got up

The girl in a pink bow

to get their fruit bowls. They preferred fibre before carbs and protein for breakfast and some caffeine afterward. They were sipping their coffees when their server from the previous night reached out to exchange a few words. He asked them to get some rest before their tour, they had to assemble in the lobby in an hour. Maohi and Javiar walked back to their room and sat on the couch. Maohi was done with her shower, so she pushed Javair into the bathroom. He pulled her in for a quickie, and she didn't know she could reach such levels of pleasure within 10 minutes. Maohi took a quick shower to wash off and then stepped out. Javiar was still shampooing his hair.

Maohi wore a beautiful yellow sundress. It had a deep neckline and elbow-length sleeves. She wore a pink bow in her hair. It was at least twice the size of the bow she was wearing the previous night and a few tones lighter. Javiar dressed in a cream co-ord set, buttoned half-sleeves shirt and knee-length shorts. He left his hair messy and wore purple aviators. He carried a Gucci Fanny pack across his chest. It was Javiar's turn to carry all the belongings. Maohi gave her credit card and her mobile to him to put in his pack.

Chapter- 28

They reached the Lobby right on time. There was only one more family, a husband and a wife with a baby girl. There were 8 more people scheduled to join, and the wine connoisseur told them that everyone would be there within 5 minutes. A husband and a wife with 2 teenagers, both glued to their phones, joined the group. The wife asked the wine connoisseur about the duration of the tour. It was evident from their accents that they were English. In the next 2 minutes, 2 more couples reached the lobby. They apologised for their delay. Both the couples were dressed in vibrant colours and were chic. All four of them knew each other and were French. The tour group was directed towards the vineyards.

The team at the vineyard gave detailed information about the different kinds of green grapes that are used for the wines. The wine connoisseur, Mark, explained how the sweetness of the wine was directly related to the harvesting. The later the grapes were harvested, the sweeter the wine. The group spent about 1 hour learning about all the grapes that were under cultivation and the harvesting schedule. They spent the next 2 hours walking around the vines and clicking pictures. The teenagers were now off their phones and listening to all the information. The only time they reached out for their gadgets was to take a picture. Javiar also walked around, capturing Maohi's fascination.

The cellar had huge oak barrels that contained different white wines. This is where they age their wines. The wine connoisseur told them about the various ingredients that went into the making of different wines. Mark also suggested different alternatives that could be added and the alternatives that don't give very good results. Just outside the cellar, there was an innovation room where different ingredients, different wood containers to age the wine and other vinification-related processes were tested. They saw 10 different barrels, 3 different kinds of wood were used to make these barrels, and each barrel had a different sample. They offered their guests the opportunity to rent a barrel for 9-12 months, based on how long they wished to age their wine before bottling it. They could choose the ingredients and select a name for the wine. Each barrel would bottle eleven bottles of wine. Two of them would be given to the guests. They would have to sign a legal contract which said that for every bottle that the hotel sold, they would get 10%. The winery would hold the rights to the wine and more such clauses were there in the contract.

Maohi and Javiar decided to create their wine, and they called it "The Pearl".

The girl in a pink bow

After the innovation room, the guests were taken to an open lawn where there were multiple buckets filled with green grapes, and 1 bucket was marked Maohi and Javiar. It was a fun activity planned for the guests on the wine tour. Maohi and javiar's bucket was marked separately because their bucket had the variant of the grape that they chose for their wine. The grape juice that would be tapped out from their crushing would be added to "The Pearl". The guests were exhausted by now, but they didn't want to miss out on this experience.

Mark took them to the pedicure salon after showing them the crushing zone. He was happy to see the relief when all the guests saw the massaging chairs with pedicure stations placed in a cute little boutique. The guests were given some time to rest while their feet were cleaned before they got onto their grape-crushing activity.

They were served refreshments, and every guest was given a thorough pedicure before they stepped into the buckets. There were 2 rows of 10 chairs each, facing in the opposite direction. The boutique was built with an elevation to ensure the views of the grape wines and the lake behind them. Each chair had a massager installed with a remote to control the massaging intensity. Guests were also served some champagne with cheese and fruits.

After an hour of pampering, they all went to their buckets. Mother and Daughter took one bucket, and father and son took the one adjacent to it. The 2 French couples switched their partners and took adjacent buckets. The family with the baby girl took 1 bucket. Maohi and Javiar got into their bucket. Everyone got busy squishing the grapes. The little girl started to jump in the bucket. The French couples who had just switched their partners seemed to be enjoying playing footsies with their new partners. Javiar held onto Maohi's waist, and she held onto his shoulders. Javair stayed put while Maohi went around jumping and crushing; he had to stabilise his goofy girlfriend. She slipped more than she squished. She eventually got tired and sat on the rim of the bucket for a little bit. Javiar took that opportunity to jump around while he held onto Maohi. It was almost 3 PM by the time guests started to step out of the bucket to wash their feet.

After cleaning their feet, Mark directed them to go to the lunch area. It was a beautiful patio between the lake and the wines in the open. The patio had a wooden deck and wooden fencing to mark the area. There were 4 tables with 4 chairs each. The servers were standing on the opposite end from the entry with trays of white wine glasses. They were handed the menu, which had the list of all the wines and they could order as many from the menu. The table chairs were wooden and painted white. The tablecloth was red and white checks. The French couples occupied one table. Girls took one side, which had the view of the lake, and the boys sat facing the girls. The couple with the teenagers took the table next to Maohi and Javiar and the last table was taken by the couple with the baby girl. Baby's mother joined 2 chairs to put her to sleep until the food came. Everyone ordered the wines that they preferred. Maohi said, "I love all of them, go ahead and order your top favourite.". They were served prawns with some aglio olio in the first round. In the second round, the servers placed lobsters and crabs on all the tables based on who ordered what.

The girl in a pink bow

By 5 PM, only the French couples and Javiar and Maohi were still seated; the others had left. Javiar wanted to order another glass of wine, and Maohi was also tempted to have another glass of the white that she had tried the previous night. They ordered a bottle of the wine that Maohi had liked from the previous night. Maohi said, "Its been a while since I felt this happy". He took her hand and kissed her. He didn't know if it was the atmosphere or the wine, but before Javiar knew it, he had told Maohi that he loved her, again. Maohi was staring wide-eyed at Javiar. She knew that she loved him, but she had not considered them being together so far. Suddenly, she was transported back to India and her culture, and she was suddenly thinking how feasible it would be for them to get married. Before she could push such a futuristic thought out of her brain, her brain played a tape of what their daughter would look like. Javiar had been sitting there, staring at her and wondering if he had said something wrong. Maohi took her 30 seconds to tell him that she loved him too.

He went down on one knee, and people started to think that he was proposing marriage. He cleared it up. "I am only asking this beautiful girl to be my girlfriend". They all awwed.

In today's world, most people want to keep themselves open to better options and where "let's go with the flow" has become the norm. A boy going down on his one knee just to ask a girl to be his girlfriend is very rare. The thought that a man wants to take full charge and control to assure that his woman feels she is the only woman for him in the entire world is breathtaking. Anything less than that is just unfortunate.

The girl in a pink bow

We all need time to understand how well we get along with our partner. We need to know the things that we are going to have to compromise on. The adjustments and the shifts needed to embrace the "Forever". Having a man wanting to commit to you and wanting to get onto this journey of exploring each other puts a woman into her feminine energy immediately. This clarity that a man can exude makes him sexier to women automatically. Situationships are meant to last a week, not weeks or months, and never a year. But unfortunately, that's all we see around ourselves. Is it the fear of missing out? Is it the hope of finding someone better? It's hard to tell.

There are 8 billion people on this planet. The chances of meeting someone better after we have committed are very high. Once we have been with someone for over a few months, we know about their shortcomings and their habits that we dislike. In this phase, if we meet someone new, he or she will be more exciting. However, we would never find out what we might end up disliking about them if we explored them romantically. There will almost always be someone outside our relationship, the idea of whom will be enticing. But we need to have the wisdom to identify that we were in the same place or maybe even in a better place a few months ago with our current partner. Choosing to stick around when it gets mundane is how we find our "ride or die".

Chapter - 29

Javiar sat next to Maohi, and they discussed the small minute details about their interactions in the last 4 months. They exchanged their stories about how they went over and beyond to ensure that they were spending time with each other without the other having a clue about how they felt. There were instances when it was Maohi's turn to prepare the dinner, as per the schedule with her MBA batchmates. She would prepare it in the afternoon and leave it in Jordan's apartment just so she could go for their swim sessions. Especially after the night they were together in the women's locker room. Maohi had promised herself that if such an opportunity presented itself, she would be bolder.

While they were sharing these stories. The boys and girls sitting next to them were making out. They noticed that Javiar and Maohi were leaving, so they offered them to join. Javiar looked at Maohi, but she chose otherwise.

The girl in a pink bow

Both Maohi and Javiar were high on love and wine, there isn't a better combination. Javiar went into the balcony to fill the jacuzzi. They enjoyed the outdoors of their suite to the fullest. Javiar got out of the Jacuzzi to light a cigarette, and Maohi stepped out to light one for herself as well. Their naked bodies were touching each other while they smoked..

They got into the bed and dozed off within 10 minutes of their heads hitting the pillow. They wanted to get some rest before they went for their champagne tasting.

Tonight, they were seated in the champagne-tasting section. Both Maohi and Javiar wanted to wind up the night early today. They just wanted to go to their room and order some pizza with coke. They just tasted 3 champagnes each and ate some from the charcuterie board and the cheese platter and were done within 60 minutes. They booked the next day's wine-tasting tour for red wines and went back to their room.

They changed into their comfortable clothes and started to watch Modern Family on the TV in the living room. It was almost midnight. Javair called for pepperoni pizza and garlic bread with some Diet Coke. Their freezer had a bucket of Ben n Jerry's Chocolate fudge brownie; they ate while they waited for their order. They had had 2 very long days; they ate their pizza and went to bed.

Chapter-30

Next morning, Maohi woke up alone in her bed. She went out to see that Javiar was going through his phone. She had completely forgotten about updating her family back in India. She took her phone out from Javiar's fanny pack. She had multiple missed calls from her mom and a list of Instagram notifications. She called her mom and spoke with her while Javiar was busy on the balcony with his phone. She went to the balcony and hugged him from behind. He turned around to kiss her on her forehead and then walked back into the living room. He told her that he wouldn't be able to make it for the wine tour today because something important at work had come up. She was disappointed, but he urged her to go on the wine tour. They woke up late and missed their breakfast, so she directly got ready to assemble at the lobby. She reached 15 minutes before time, and luckily for her, the breakfast was still open. She took some fruits and French toast with coffee. There was a group of girls on this tour, she luckily got some company to

The girl in a pink bow

make small talk. She called him to at least come for the grape crushing, but he didn't answer. Maohi chose to sit out of it herself as well. She kept missing him and sending him texts. He didn't respond. When it was time for lunch and she asked him to come to the new venue where they were serving red wines, he again didn't answer.

Now she was starting to worry; she knew that he looked distant and worried in the morning. Maohi didn't want to pester him, so she didn't enquire further. But now that he hadn't replied to any of her texts, nor had he answered her calls, she had lost all her appetite, so she left mid-lunch to go back to her room. She rang the bell, but no one answered. She opened the door of the room with her key.

She entered the room and there was no sign of him, she was shocked to see that his stuff was gone. He had just left a post-it on the fridge.

"I am sorry I can't do this. I have booked a cab for you in the morning. You will be dropped at the train station. Your return train ticket is in your mailbox. You can take the train from Union Station back to the campus. I will be spending few days in downtown"

Maohi collapsed on the floor, she didn't know what had happened. She had no idea. She called him a million times, and he didn't answer. She cried her eyes out throughout the evening. She passed out crying on her couch in the living room. She woke up, and it was all dark. She hoped that it was all a dream and when she turned on the lights, Javiar would still be in the room but he was nowhere to be seen. She took a hot

The girl in a pink bow

water shower and called Suvreen and all the others to talk to them, and they all pacified her. She ordered some food for herself and started to pack. She couldn't bear the thought of continuing Modern Family from where they had left it the previous night. She blamed herself for letting him trick her into believing that he was not a fuck-boy. She played friends and ate Biryani. She needed Indian food to feel better. Comfort food helps us get through our bad days. Though Maohi's first preference was rajma chawal, she settled on the closest thing available. Once she was fed, she called her mother to distract herself. They spoke for an hour, and then she fell asleep. She didn't want to be conscious for whatever time she was left with to be in the hotel. Every nook and cranny reminded her of Javiar and their time together.

Maohi woke up at 5 AM, and she decided to check out of her room immediately. She collected her luggage and went to the reception desk. Her transport to the railway station was booked for 8 AM. She spent the next 3 hours in the breakfast area, reading and eating. She took her taxi at 8 AM, and by evening, she was back in her campus apartment. She fixed herself a mug of coffee and sat on the balcony with Suvreen.

There isn't enough that one can say about having good girlfriends in our lives. Female friendships are an integral part of a girl's life. All we need is a 2-3 hour conversation over coffee and some chocolate cookies. Maohi felt lighter after talking her heart out. They both tried to figure out what went wrong. The only possible option was that he proposed under the influence of liquor but freaked out the following morning. The moment the gravity of the situation hit him, he ran because he wasn't ready for any serious commitment. They ruled out the thought of him using her only for a fun weekend. He wouldn't put their friendship in jeopardy for something so silly. Though Maohi argued against it, she thought that he probably was using her all this time. He needed someone to rely on academically. She was available, and they had common subjects. Suvreen argued that he would have preferred to have Maohi as academic support for their last term as well; they still could have had overlapping subjects. Maohi was convinced when Suvreen pointed out that he had enough options for a fun weekend; he was famous with the girls.

Maohi went to bed. She spent her Wednesday tucked in, watching Twilight series. It was a rainy day, and she hadn't even begun to recover from her heartbreak. But today, somehow, she felt lighter. She preferred sunny days but she was too tired to be her happy self. The clouds gave her a day off from being joyful all the time. She ate maggi tucked into her flamingo blanket and watched Bella uncover Edward Cullen's secret. By the time she reached the point where Jacob transformed into a werewolf, she started to wonder if Javiar was a mystical creature. That he was not responding to mails but checking the weather forecast every morning and since today it was supposed to be raining he couldn't be with her. Maybe, somehow, what sun was to Edward, rain was to Javiar. Is he a vampire? Is he an Alien? Does he need the sun to function?

A broken heart seeks answers and comfort in the oddest of places. We try to connect the dots and validate our feelings. It's a shrewd world. We hear people getting violated all the time. People get played on and cheated on by their partners all the time. We know that it happens around us, but we struggle to accept it when we are at the receiving end. It could be a sense of entitlement or superiority complex or both or neither or something else completely, but when we are grieving, we give ourselves the benefit of the doubt. "It couldn't have happened to me". Pragmatism is important to heal but delusion is an effective balm when grieving.

After 2 minutes of entertaining her irrational thoughts, she went back to her movie.

Chapter - 31

Maohi spent all of her summer working. Though she had planned to travel at least every alternate weekend, she ended up taking just one trip to Wasaga Beach with her friends. She spent most of her time working. Her office was downtown and she went to work even on the days she could have chosen to work from home.

Mehul played soccer with Javiar's flatmates. Since Javiar's and Mehul's penthouses were adjacent to each other. Javiar's flatmates had become good friends with Mehul. They played soccer almost every weekend. Every time Mehul's penthouse hosted dinner or a game night, Maohi got some information about Javiar from his flatmates. The nights she came back after a few beers and some information on Javiar, she cried herself to sleep. Initially, she would end up calling Javiar, but he never responded, nor did he ever reply to her texts. He was never on the list of her Instagram story views. She knew he was active on Instagram because he was always on the Instagram story

The girl in a pink bow

viewer's list of her batchmates. She figured that he had muted her.

All she knew about him was that he was living in Downtown with some girl. She assumed it was the girl he spent the night with. He would rarely entertain his friends. He didn't speak to anyone because he was very, very busy with his work. She thought that he probably got together with his old flame. She started to think that maybe it was her who had texted him the other morning and he was running back to her. Probably, that is why he wanted to stay in downtown. Any mention of Javiar would impact her negatively. It wasn't that Maohi had come even close to moving on, but she preferred to stay distracted from any thought of him. She slowly stopped attending the penthouse parties. She focused on her work and staying outdoors. Maohi would go out for picnic dates with Suvreen on the weekends. She went for her coffee runs with Mehul whenever they both were free.

Before she knew it, it was time for her last term. The leaves were changing colors, and the days were getting shorter.

Mehul and Jordan planned pizzas and beers in the penthouse with everyone. They assured her that their neighbours wouldn't be crashing the party. Summer was almost done, and she had sworn off alcohol. One night Maohi drank a bit too much and she called Javiar 100 times. She was so ashamed and embarrassed of herself the next morning that she decided to quit until she felt better again. It had been 2 months since, and she had started to feel better. She hadn't healed completely, but she was in a better place both emotionally and mentally. She wanted to enjoy a few chilled beers before the weather got harsh.

The girl in a pink bow

Mehul prepared fancy dips for crackers, and Jordan got beers. Maohi set up the balcony with speakers, fairy lights and bean bags.

They saw the sunset and the city lights come up before they ordered their pizza. All of them discussed the subjects they had chosen for the last semester. Each of them needed only 4 subjects to complete their credits. Mikhail proposed to continue with their cooking arrangement and everyone agreed. Maohi had classes only on Mondays and Wednesdays. So she chose Tuesday and Thursday.

It started to get chilly, so they moved their party indoors. They spoke about their first summer in Canada and the things they did. After a long time, Maohi was interacting with her batchmates without the agenda of finding out more about Javiar. She hadn't laughed so much in a very long time. She wasn't particularly sad, but nothing gave her joy. Tonight, she felt that she was getting a part of herself back. A part that had gone somewhere in the hiding. Her laughter finally reached her eyes. Jordan told her that she was starting to laugh with her eyes again.

It was almost midnight, past Maohi's bedtime. Maohi was a night owl but because she had to commute for an hour every morning to get to work, she had brought in some alterations in her sleep cycle. She left the penthouse to go back to her room. The moment she turned towards the elevators, she bumped into Javiar. They looked at each other for a second. Maohi had no patience to wait for the elevator, so she ran towards the fire exit. She didn't look back and started climbing down. She got into a different elevator on the next floor. Her heart was racing, and she was breathing frantically. She covered her face with her hands and started to yell. "This is not fair!" "This is not fair!" "I was getting better" "No, no, no, no". By the time she reached her apartment, she had tears running down her eyes. She rushed into her bathroom and splashed cold water on her face until she calmed down.

Then she got into her bed and played light music. She was all cried out. She caught herself smiling before she drifted away to sleep. She knew she was royally fucked but Javiar was back.

Maohi started frequenting Mehul's penthouse in hopes of running into Javiar again. Mehul told her that he never came for any of the games and he barely saw Javiar. Maohi started to go to the common laundry room more frequently. Every time she stepped out of her apartment, she hoped to run into him. She spent all of her fall hoping to run into him. Her term ended. Neither did she see him in any of her classes, nor did she ever see him again after that night. Her batchmates from the penthouse ran into him once or twice throughout the fall term. He was in the building, but their paths never crossed. Maohi accepted it as her fate and a sign from the universe. No matter the proximity or the connection, they weren't meant to be.

Once again, it was term end, every apartment was celebrating and it was a replay of the night she and Javiar had kissed for the first time. Maohi had decided not to be a part of it this time. She submitted her last assignment by 8 PM because she had a train to catch at 10 PM.

The girl in a pink bow

The day she found herself stepping out of the apartment for the 10th time in the hopes of running into Javiar, she decided to get rid of this madness. She booked herself a solo trip to Montreal on the day of her last submission. She spent all her time being ahead on her project work and assignments so she would be able to complete her last submission before time. Apart from that, she spent her free time researching and planning for Montreal. This was going to be her first solo trip.

She was all packed a day before. Maohi submitted her assignment before 8 PM and was on the metro to the Union Station by 8: 30 PM. She had booked an overnight train to Montreal.

Chapter - 32

She reached Montreal at 6 in the morning. It was a December morning. It had snowed the previous night, but now it was bright and sunny. Her hostel check-in was at 11 AM. She found a bakery, 200 metres from her hostel and decided to wait there. She had her coffee, charged her phone and ate her breakfast. Maohi had travelled alone a lot of times but never for a holiday. Up until now, it was all very familiar. She was used to being by herself at airports, bus stops, train stations, and cafes. She always carried her eye mask and a book. She slept when she could, and when she couldn't, she read. Though she hadn't slept that well the previous night, now, since she was waiting for her check-in, she chose to drain her sleep in coffee and kill her time by reading "Heresy". Maohi was obsessed with Giordano Bruno.

She checked into her hostel. Maohi was allotted the upper bunk bed. 4 boys were sleeping on the opposite beds, and a girl was busy on her laptop in the bed below her. There were 2 more

The girl in a pink bow

girls in the adjacent bed. They had checked in with Maohi as well. Maohi hadn't booked her return ticket because it was her first time on a holiday by herself; she didn't know what to expect. Since she had no fear of losing the number of days she had. She chose to catch some sleep.

She plugged in her earphones and picked a random pink noise. Then she put on her eye mask and drifted into a deep sleep.

She woke up to the four boys chatting. They apologised to her but it was too late. She gave them a passive-aggressive smile that made them laugh sheepishly and apologetically. They introduced themselves to her. They were travelling from San Francisco. One of them said, "December in Montreal is magical. Once all the Christmas decorations are up, it looks like a winter heaven". It doesn't really snow in San Francisco, so they had come to Montreal for a snowy Christmas and a European vibe. They invited her to have dinner with them. They had heard about a little pub that was playing 90's commercial tonight. Maohi, being a 90s kid, was immediately excited about it. She was relieved that she wouldn't have to be by herself, at least for her first evening. She wore a short gray dress with a long brown coat and black boots. She wore red lipstick and pinned a pink bow in her hair.

They all went to the club and sang along loudly to 90's pop. Maohi ordered a poutine with some ginger ale. They bought her 2 shots of tequila as an apology for disturbing her nap. She graciously accepted. They all sang and danced on the tables until the bar shut down. All of them walked back to their hostel, singing and dancing. Maohi had never felt so liberated. She

The girl in a pink bow

wasn't sure if her decision was wise, but she was glad that at least her first night was worth the courage she had to foster.

She went in for a quick shower and changed into her night suit. By the time she came back, all the lights were out, and everyone had slept. She used her iPhone's torch to look for her charger in her bag. The moment she unzipped her bag, she found a note.

"The Girl in a pink bow - You wear happiness and laughter like no one. I watched you be yourself all night, and I could have watched more without blinking."

Maohi wondered which of the 4 boys had slipped in the note. She was nursing a heartache and wasn't ready for anything romantic. Though the boys were cute, they were way younger. She didn't wish to analyse this note any further. She was elated to find out how loudly her happiness was radiating out of her. A little attention and solid proof that she was happy was enough for her for tonight. She folded the note and kept it in her bag. She climbed onto her bed and slept.

Now that her MBA was done, she had to start searching for jobs. Maohi had decided to spend 1 hour every day, after her coffee and breakfast, applying for jobs. She sat in the small corner of a coffee shop. It was a quiet zone in a sunlit corner surrounded by books. She got herself her second mug of coffee and started with her job applications. After an hour of dedication, she got up to stretch and went into her dorm. Maohi changed into a woollen cord set with a Christmas sweater. She decided to explore the botanical garden, which had a good collection of bonsai. She stepped out of her dorm and then

The girl in a pink bow

came running back. She had forgotten to put on her pink bow. It had become her security blanket. Javiar's ghosting had driven Maohi into a lot of self-doubt. She was starting to feel as if she wasn't enough. Whenever she stalked his old flame living in Toronto, she felt horrible about herself. Melissa looked like a Vogue Model. This pink bow was a reminder of the note she got, she had been craving that kind of validation for a while now. Pinning that bow was equivalent to wearing a crown.

She bought a bonsai tree from the botanical garden and placed it on her bedside. Every bed had a small rack above the charging point, so she placed it there. She hadn't seen the 4 boys from last night all day today. The girl in the lower bunk asked her if she wanted to go out for a girls' night. All the girls in the dorm had decided to over-dress and go to the Crescent Street for tonight. Maohi couldn't have been more excited about it. She wanted to take a power nap before she got dressed. All the girls stepped out at 7 PM, that's when she bumped into the San Francisco boys. Sam tried to make small talk, She wondered if he was the one out of the four who put the note in her bag.

The girl under Maohi's bunk was Maria from Russia. She had been travelling solo for the past 1 month. Maria was a 32-year-old Software Developer. She had recently quit her job to travel the world. She wanted to relocate out of Russia, so she decided to go on a solo expedition to find herself a place of her liking. She had liked Puerto Rico so far.

All the girls were dressed in sexy black dresses. Maohi wore the one from her quarantine time, the one she almost wore for her Christmas date with Leo. Of course, she wasn't going to step out without her pink bow. She did her hair up in a tight bun and put a tiny clip with a small pink bow on the side to keep her bun steady. She looked extra sexy with her hair up in the tube dress. She wore red panties, every time her dress's slit shifted upward it flashed a red string. She wore a long grey coat with black heeled boots.

Four of them club hopped all night. They got enough male attention, but both Maria and Maohi wanted to keep their distance from the Y chromosome. They shared a moment in the ladies room. It was first time for both of them, so they enjoyed exploring. They decided not to kiss because Maohi had just done her lipstick. They came out of the stall, giggling and joined the other 2. Maohi and Maria kept playfully touching each other throughout the night.

Maohi climbed back up to her bed and 5 minutes later, Maria joined her. They spent an hour together under the sheets. Maria went back to her bed and they both fell asleep. Though it was a fun experiment, they both got back to bed knowing that they were as straight as they come. Maybe just bi-curious.

Maria and Maohi met for breakfast the next morning but there was no awkwardness. Maohi loved Maria's company and she hoped to share the bunk bed with her for at least a week. She got down to her job applications after her meal. Maohi had to buy a diary and a pen to make notes on her job applications. She went back to her dorm to get her credit card from her bag. She found another note.

"The Girl in a pink bow - You looked gorgeously naughty. Your carefree compliments your sexy!"

Maohi had put a face to these notes. She was almost sure that it was Sam's handwriting on the notes. He was too young for her. The notes were harmless and cute, so she decided not to do anything about it. She had no interest in acting upon it but having an admirer helped her repair her bruised self-esteem.

Chapter - 33

It was Maohi's 3rd day in Montreal, Maria had to go meet a friend. So she decided to spend the day relaxing and watching a movie. She stayed in all day and stepped out to get herself a pizza slice in the evening. Her hostel's street had cafes, restaurants and some stores. She got herself coffee from the bakery she waited in on her first day before her check-in and then went to a small takeaway pizza joint. On her way back, the owner of the bakery came out to return her book that she had forgotten there. She opened the book to find another note.

"The Girl in a pink bow - I dreamt of you last night. We were building sand castles. I spent the entire day daydreaming about what it would be like to build sand castles together."

Though all of Sam's friends had gone out today, he stayed back. He was working on his laptop all day. Maohi had anticipated that he would stay back for her. When she went back to her hostel, he was nowhere to be seen. The boys had

The girl in a pink bow

left to get dinner. She thought he would have followed her to the coffee shop and then slid the note. It was just Maohi and 2 girls in her adjacent bunk bed. They shared a few stories from their night on Crescent Street. Maohi kept her little adventure with Maria under wraps. All of them decided to call it a night.

Maohi woke up to pee in the middle of the night. She opened the door and was shocked to find Sam with another boy. She immediately closed the door and went back to her bed. She stayed awake for the next one hour, holding her bladder and freaking out about her secret admirer. She heard Sam come back and went to use the loo immediately. She ran into the boy Sam was with on her way to the loo. He wasn't one of the other 3 San Francisco boys.

Maohi decided to be a little more observant of her surroundings the following day. She could be getting into some trouble with a stalker. She temporarily entertained the thought of Maria sliding in the notes. But her doubt was cleared when Maria told her that she had gone out on a Tinder date the other night and it was not to meet an old friend. Maohi was a little confused when Maria randomly shared her location with her. She thought that she did it by mistake but Maria was just being careful.

Maohi and the girls had decided to go to the Montreal Museum of Fine Arts. They dressed up in fancy outfits and it looked like the cast of "sex and the City" - Four girls walking around in Crescent Street, looking for a cab to go to the museum. They had coffees in one hand and small bites like muffins, bagels etc in the other. Maohi was adamant about

The girl in a pink bow

finding her secret admirer. She had told her friends about the notes and they were all on the lookout to catch him.

They entered the museum together and 20 minutes into their tour, they were all scattered around in different corners. Maohi sat down and removed her red heels. She was tired of walking around in them. It was a huge museum, not a place for an amateur in heels.

There was a note placed next to her, she knew what it was. She picked it up and started to look around. A man was walking away, he was taking very fast steps for someone at a museum. Maohi started to run towards him barefoot. Her red stilettos banged into one of the art pieces, and she attracted attention. The man started to run, he realised that he was being followed. Maohi started shouting in the museum "stop the man in the lavender sweater and blue jeans, he is a stalker!"

Chapter - 34

The security guards ran towards him, so the stalker stopped running. Javiar turned to face Maohi, and she couldn't believe her eyes. It occurred to her why the handwriting was familiar. She had blocked out the vineyard so hard that it never crossed her mind. The post-it note left behind by Javiar had the same "i"s as in the notes that she had been receiving. The security guards arrested him but Maohi refused to identify him.

They were taken into a small room where Javiar explained that she was his estranged girlfriend and he was just trying to win her back. Maohi sat there, disagreeing to make his life difficult. Javiar took his phone out and shared all of their photos and his University ID card. The security guards looked at Maohi with a straight face, expecting her to drop the charges and accept his claim. She rolled her eyes at them and walked out.

The girl in a pink bow

They opened Javiar's handcuffs. He looked at the police officers. "Merci beaucoup, Enchante!"

He ran behind Maohi. She was nowhere to be seen, he thought he lost her. He went out and saw her get into a cab. He got a cab and asked the driver to follow her. They reached her hostel, and Maohi ran into her dorm. He was stopped at the gate since he wasn't a guest at the hostel. He kept saying that he was here to see a friend. Maohi kept denying that she knew him. He was forced to book a bed just so that he could speak to her.

Javiar apologised for his behaviour. Maohi was furious, and tears of rage started to run down her cheeks. She wasn't willing to hear him out. Javiar begged her to just give him one chance to explain himself. Maohi wouldn't look at him, but he started to talk anyway.

"The morning after I proposed, I woke up to make coffee for us. After turning on the coffee maker, I sat down to check my mails. I opened my fanny pack and it had your phone in it. I didn't intend to see anything but there were messages from Leo. I saw the notifications on your screen"

Maohi opened her Instagram to check Leonardo's messages.

Leonard:

"It is so nice to hear from you."

"Let's meet soon?"

"I know you felt something the other night because I felt it too."

The girl in a pink bow

"My girlfriend and I are on a break."

"Call me."

"See you!"

Maohi had completely forgotten about Leo. She never saw the notifications from him because she immediately called her mother that morning. She saw the last message from Leo in her message list and assumed "See you!" was a conversation wrap. She hadn't opened the texts up until now. Javiar was relieved to see that Maohi hadn't seen the texts.

Javiar explained to Maohi that he was avoiding running into her or any of her friends because he was embarrassed. He thought Maohi was involved in some capacity with Leonardo. Maohi had told Javiar about what had happened during Quarantine, and he knew that she was obsessing over him viewing her Insta stories. Eventually, that faded away, and Javiar was relieved. But that morning, when he saw those notifications on her screen, he was heartbroken. He didn't want to confront Maohi because he knew that he would believe whatever story Maohi told him. He didn't want to be lied to.

Maohi asked him about the millions of attempts she had made to reach out to him. Javiar was furious and hurting; he didn't want anything to do with her. On the night of their last submissions, he ran into Suvreen. Suvreen and him got into some small talk and Suvreen gave it off to him. Javiar found out from Suvreen that Leo and Maohi were never in touch. Suvreen told him about how deeply Maohi was into him and what the last 8 months were like for her.

The girl in a pink bow

Javiar took whatever details he could from Suvreen about Maohi's travel plans, and he got onto the next bus to Montreal. He saw her going out to the club with the boys. Javiar didn't know what to say, he followed her and saw her dancing and singing. He said, "You were too happy to be disturbed. Suvreen told me how upset you had been. I didn't want to upset you." So he just slid a note in her bag. He followed her to the botanical garden and almost got caught trying to slide a note into her bag while she was busy choosing the Bonsai she wanted to buy.

Javiar waited every day for her to step out and he followed her. He just wanted to find the right moment to speak to her. He followed her on the night of her bar hopping because he had failed to give her his note for the day. Javiar managed to slide it into her bag when she was ordering at one of the bars. He joked, "I saw you getting handsy with the other chick. I thought maybe you switched teams." He wondered if he had hurt her so bad that she swore off men. "I had to change my note, You were being a naughty girl." He had decided to come clean to her today. Maohi opened the note again to read it.

"The girl in a pink bow - Please forgive me, I have made a huge mistake. If you can give me one chance to explain myself, meet me at Notre Dame tomorrow at 12 noon - Javiar Diaz".

Maohi tore that note and took out all the other notes and tore them as well. She asked him to leave and to never see her again. She felt that not only had he betrayed her but he had doubted her morality too. She didn't want to be with someone who would not put in the effort to at least make an attempt to try and find out the truth.

The girl in a pink bow

Javiar left. He had anticipated this but was hoping otherwise. Maria and the other girls walked in just when Javiar left. Maohi was in tears, she narrated what had happened. It was dark outside and all of them cancelled their dinner plans to be with her. Sam entered with his boys and saw the estrogen overflowing in the dorm. The boys tried to lighten up the mood. Maria advised her to sleep over it. She could tell that it had been an overwhelming day for Maohi. Maohi was too tired, mentally and physically, so she agreed to it. They all cancelled their dinner plans and stayed in with her to play board games, card games, dumb charades, etc.

The friendships and the bonds that we build when we are travelling are one of a kind. These fellow travelers don't have any image of who we were in the past, they meet us as who we are in that phase. That is why we feel that sometimes strangers understand us better. We wonder how that can be. It's easier for them to do so because they have not interacted with the earlier versions of us. Also, we have much fewer apprehensions about being judged. We don't mind being who we truly are.

The next morning, Maria sat next to Maohi. She nudged her to think about her situation and try to see things from Javiar's perspective. She said, "One broken heart took an extreme step in Niagara. Maybe another broken heart can choose to be wise in Montreal". Maohi smiled and hugged Maria. She had been contemplating the same, she wanted to hear someone else say it. Maohi didn't want to be a fool in love. Maria reassured her that she wasn't being one.

Javiar's phone was switched off. Maohi didn't know if he would show up at Notre Dame at noon, but that was the fastest

The girl in a pink bow

way to meet him. Maohi dressed up and booked her cab. It was snowing. She reached Notre Dame by 12:05 PM. She ran up the stairs in the snow and into the cathedral. He was sitting there, praying. He opened his eyes, and there she saw. Maohi twirled to show him her pink bow. He laughed and said, "Remind me to wish for 100 billion dollars when we are here the next time. My last wish was granted immediately."

They walked out of the cathedral. The snow, the cobblestone footpath, the Christmas decoration and 2 estranged lovers, it was a scene from a christmas romcom. Javiar took Maohi to "Restaurant Bonaparte". He had booked a romantic lunch for the two of them. The moment they were seated, she was presented with a cake. "Happy Birth -1 day Love". It was Maohi's birthday eve tonight, she hadn't told anyone but Javiar remembered.

She wanted to be by herself for her birthday. She had decided to take herself out on a romantic date in Montreal. There were times when she pictured herself cutting the cake and toasting a glass of wine like a boss-girl, but there were also times she pictured herself weeping all by herself with a cake in front of her and the candle melting on the cake. People pitying her and the server finally blowing out the candle to avoid the melting wax from becoming the frosting on the cake.

But she wasn't going to be alone. Javiar had booked them on a flight to Cancun for her Birthday. They cut their lunch date short to a slice of cake and a cup of coffee and rushed to the airport. Maria sent her luggage directly to the airport. He had booked them on a business class flight. They checked in by 2 PM and continued their lunch date in the business class

The girl in a pink bow

lounge. They boarded the flight by 5:35 PM and landed in Cancun at 10:45 PM. It was midnight by the time they collected their luggage and booked their cab. Javiar was dancing and mouthing "Birthday Sex, Birthday Sex" By Jeremih.

They checked into an all-inclusive resort and their villa had its own private little beach. Maohi and Javaiar hadn't been intimate in 8 months. They were both aching to put an end to this dry spell. They quickly undressed themselves and spent the entire night in each other's embrace.

They woke up in the morning and went for a swim in the ocean and then went for their breakfast. Javiar had to go for a meeting with a client who was doing a photoshoot for a newly launched swimwear collection of a luxury brand. He left for his meeting and Maohi decided to explore the property. After 30 minutes of exploring the resort and its facilities, she carried her beach towel and a book and decided to spend the rest of her morning reading on the beach. She sat down on the white sand, facing the turquoise blue ocean in her yellow bikini. She sipped her coffee and took out a novel from her bag.

www.ingramcontent.com/pod-product-compliance
Lightning Source LLC
LaVergne TN
LVHW041937070526
838199LV00051BA/2822